Charles P. Kirkland

The Destiny of our Country

Charles P. Kirkland

The Destiny of our Country

ISBN/EAN: 9783337235468

Printed in Europe, USA, Canada, Australia, Japan

Cover: Foto ©Andreas Hilbeck / pixelio.de

More available books at **www.hansebooks.com**

THE

DESTINY

OF

OUR COUNTRY.

CHARLES P. KIRKLAND.

NEW YORK:
PUBLISHED BY ANSON D. F. RANDOLPH,
No. 770 BROADWAY.
1864.

PREFATORY NOTE.

I was invited by the "Association of Alumni" of Hamilton College, N. Y., to deliver an address at their annual meeting on the 20th of July, 1864. The following paper was prepared pursuant to that invitation. The portion relating to matters merely local and personal is now omitted. Much was omitted, for want of time, on the delivery. Some notes are added. The address is published by request.

CHARLES P. KIRKLAND.

New York, July, 1864.

THE DESTINY OF OUR COUNTRY.

In 1816, when, reckoning our national life from the time of the recognition by Great Britain of our Independence, we had existed as a people but thirty-three years, we had recently emerged from a three years' war with the most powerful nation on the globe; our commercial and other material interests had suffered the natural consequences of war; a national debt, large for that period, and certainly large for a nation of our then "tender years," had been incurred; that war had been conducted, not only against our external foe, but against the opposition of an influential minority at home, yet not many years elapsed before we recovered from the calamities of that conflict; our war debt was extinguished, and we started again on our former course of national prosperity, greatness and glory, with a future before us of more splendid promise than was ever before presented to any people.

It would seem as if all lovers of that civil and religious liberty secured by our form of government, whether citizens of our own Republic, or dwellers under other and unfriendly systems, had the full assurance of the realization of their most ardent hopes and aspirations, and that here was indeed erected a "Temple of Liberty," in which all of any nationality, who desired to worship at her shrine, would for ever find welcome and protection; and that that edifice, erected by our fathers, and thus far sacredly preserved by their successors, was destined to fall only when "the last trumpet should sound," and when should be heard the solemn and final fiat for the destruction of all things on earth. Occasionally, indeed, clouds were seen in the horizon, and mutterings as of a storm were heard in the distance; but the former were dispelled and the latter silenced under the influence of the attachment of our people to their institutions, energized and vitalized, on one occasion especially, by the strong-minded, the iron-willed and the ever-loyal Jackson.

For more than seventy years after the adoption of the Constitu-

tion, no event occurred seriously threatening the peaceful progress
of our country toward its destined place at the head, in respect of
population and of national and moral power, of the nations of the
world.   So strong and so abiding had our faith become in the impossibility of any serious attack on, or of any real danger to, the
the ever-blessed Union of the States, that after all the threatening
acts and declarations at Washington and elsewhere, prior to the
Presidential election in 1860, watchful, and discriminating, and experienced men entertained not the slightest imagination that the
country was in peril, or that any overt, actual attempt would, or
even *could*, be made to subvert the Government.   Not four weeks
prior to that election, I was assured by a distinguished representa-
tive of this State in the Senate of the United States, and who was
then, and for many years had been, an influential and attentive
member of that body, that the country need have no fears, for, that
after the election, matters would subside into their usual quiet, and
the last thing there was cause for apprehending was an actual attempt to dissolve the Union.   A very few weeks after that election, another eminent Senator from our State emphatically declared,
in a large public assemblage, that before the lapse of sixty days all
vestiges of public opposition to the Government would disappear.

In the views thus expressed by the persons to whom I allude, we
see the confirmation of the remark just made, that the great body of
our people had come to regard it as a practical impossibility that
any portion of our own citizens would ever lay violent hands on
our political structure with a serious view to its demolition.   It
seemed impossible and incredible, after the beneficent operation of
our institutions and the brilliant career of our country for so many
years, that any considerable number could be found within its
bosom, willing and prepared to consign it to a speedy and an everlasting death.   Yet this revolting spectacle has been witnessed, and
the close of the year 1860 exhibited to our almost unbelieving eyes,
and to astonished Europe, the deliberate inauguration of a series of
measures, intended for the express and terrible purpose of the overthrow of the Government and the dissolution of the Union.   The
reality and depth and desperateness of that purpose have since
been frightfully demonstrated.   The first gun fired at Fort Sumter
on the 12th of April, 1861, informed us, in language not to be mistaken, that a civil war with all its horrors was upon us; it fore-
boded scenes of carnage and desolation and death not equalled in

all previous history ; and all that was then imagined by the most vivid and apprehensive fancy has found its awful reality within the three years that have elapsed since that never to be forgotten day.

The contest then and thus commenced is yet pending ; it enlists, as well it may, the earnest and the anxious interest of all patriots here and of all lovers of civil liberty everywhere; all such look with unspeakable solicitude to the future.

Under these solemn circumstances, I know of no theme more appropriate for the consideration of American citizens than "The Destiny of our Country."

The consideration of this subject of necessity involves an inquiry into the causes of the present rebellion, its true nature and character, and its intended, and, if successful, its inevitable effects ; whether it can be successful, and if not, the position in which the several States, those in rebellion and those not in rebellion, will be at the time of its overthrow, the mode in which the States in rebellion will resume their former position in the Union ; and then, the future of our country. In such an inquiry it is obvious that every thought and every feeling of what may be denominated "*party*," in its technical and restricted sense must be absolutely banished; "abolitionists," "republicans," "democrats," as representing party ideas and party organizations, must all and equally be ignored.

I.

The first overt act of treason and rebellion was in December, 1860, when at Columbia, in South Carolina, one hundred and sixty-nine citizens of that State assembled, called themselves a Convention of the people of the State, adjourned to Charleston, and there, on the 21st day of that month, adopted an "ordinance" (as they termed it) of secession from the Union. This example was almost immediately followed in the remaining rebel States, and in such a manner as conclusively to show that this act in that State was the premeditated act of the leading spirits of the rebellion throughout those States,* and was, to all practical purposes, its commencement—

---

* It is a significant fact, that the Governors at that time (1860-'61) of five of the rebel States were natives of South Carolina—had been "brought up at the feet" of her "Gamaliel," and were deeply imbued with those fatal political heresies which contributed so much to bring upon our country her present dire calamities.

its birth. It is vitally important in this branch of the inquiry to advert to the then condition of our country in general, and of the rebel States in particular. The general condition of the Republic, as has already been stated, was a condition of unexampled prosperity; we had then existed as an independent people, dating from the Declaration of Independence, eighty-four years, and from the adoption of the Constitution, seventy-one years, and neither ancient nor modern times furnish any example of so wonderful a national advance, in so brief a period, in glory, honor, and material and moral power. Our prosperity excited the admiration of all who loved, and the ill-will and envy of all who hated, free institutions. The most sanguine and enthusiastic of the men of the Revolution and of the Convention of 1787, never anticipated from their labors such magnificent results in so short a time. In all this glory, honor, prosperity and power, the people of the rebel States were full and welcome participants. The sun never shone on political communities in the more perfect enjoyment of civil and religious liberty; of social, personal, and domestic security; of entire protection in the possession and use of all their property of every kind; and of more material prosperity and of more exalted *national* glory and prestige than were the people of the ten rebel States on the 1st day of December, 1860.

Those States, too, up to that day had been the favored and the petted sisters of the family; with less than one-third of the population, wealth and business resources of the Republic, they had, up to that time, been the recipients of nearly two-thirds of its highest and valuable offices, as will be seen by an examination of the list of our Presidents and Vice-Presidents, Cabinet and Foreign Ministers, and Army and Navy officers. They had had, in profuse liberality, and wholly in disproportion to their contributions to the public treasury, appropriations for forts, harbors, custom houses, post offices, internal navigation, mail facilities and many other public objects. They had never failed to have a preponderating power in the national Congress; and at the election of President Lincoln, and at the very moment of the rebellion, the Senate and House of Representatives contained a majority politically opposed to him and sympathizing, in all that was *possible under the Constitution*, with the South.

Up to the period in question (December 1, 1860), the most painstaking and hypercritical scrutiny will fail to discover a solitary act, on the part of the Government of the United States, of hostility, or even of unkindness or discourtesy, toward those States or their people. On the contrary, authentic history shows that the national Government had uniformly exhibited to those States, their people and their institutions, marked kindness, indulgence, and, it may almost be said, partiality. No intelligent, candid, foreign observer could fail to perceive that, as between the North and the South, the latter had been from the start the marked favorite of the General Government. Unquestionably, for many years *individuals* at the North, technically known as " *Abolitionists*,"* had orally and in print uttered sentiments adverse alike to the " peculiar institution" of the South and to the Constitution of their country ; but it is equally unquestionable that those individuals were few in number, insignificant in influence and absurdly fanatical in character. The paucity of their numbers and their utter destitution of influence were conclusively demonstrated at the New York election in November, 1860, when their candidate for Governor, out of the 700,000 electors of the State, received but 5,000 votes, about one in one hundred and fifty of the voting population. It is true, too, that during the same period, the Legislatures of two or three of the Northern States had passed acts intended to obstruct the operation of the " Fugitive Slave" law ; but those acts, under the influence of the popular feeling at the North, were repealed before the inauguration of the rebellion, and had they not been, they would have been adjudged void by the supreme judicial tribunal of the Union as in direct violation of the Constitution of the United States. These expressions of individual sentiment, as above stated, can never be restrained in a country where liberty of speech and of the press are of the very birthright of the citizen ; and it is in place here to say, that in view of the fatal dangers which, for the last thirty years, have attended the promulgation of such sentiments in any Southern State, they have had no utterance there. It may be said, without fear of contradiction, that during the whole time of the existence on the statute book of the State laws just mentioned, they were practically inoperative, and that not a single fugitive escaped a return to his master by means of their provisions. No unprejudiced and reasonably well-informed man, whether a dweller in the Northern or in the Southern States, or in a foreign country, can in his heart believe that the sayings or the doings of

* What I mean by this term is stated in a subsequent note.

" Abolitionists," or the State laws above mentioned, have ever, to any perceptible degree, affected the safety, the domestic tranquillity or the pecuniary interests of the citizens of any Southern State. Certainly, no sane man will assert that the slightest danger or detriment in any manner has thereby arisen to any State *south of the border slave States ;* and yet the latter, which are the only States practically exposed to any trouble or injury from the causes I have mentioned, have not (with the exception of Eastern Virginia,) united in the rebellion.

It is unnecessary to dwell on these matters; my purpose in this branch of the subject is to present in a clear and vivid light, such as the truth justifies and requires, the great and undeniable fact, that up to the time of the breaking out of the rebellion the history of our Government presents not a solitary act of aggression on the rights, the material interests, the domestic security and tranquility of the people of any rebel State, or of any portion thereof. In an inquiry as to the motives and causes of the rebellion and its nature and character, it is not possible to overestimate or to overstate the importance of the *truth*, in the first place as to the actual condition of those States in reference to all that constitutes the happiness, the security, the prosperity of a community, at the time of their first overt act in the scheme for the overthrow of the Government of their country ; and, in the second place, as to the treatment they had invariably received from that Government from the first hour of its existence up to that momentous day. It is, indeed, impossible for any one to arrive at just conclusions as to the merits of the tremendous conflict now existing without a knowledge and appreciation of the *truth* as to the two matters just mentioned ; and when the honest inquirer, whether he belongs to one party, or another, or to no party, shall have made the inquiry and investigation necessary to convince him what that *truth* is, he will inevitably arrive at the result I have stated and at that result only. It is the result necessarily produced by the irrefragable testimony of admitted fact and of undisputed history. Before the conclusion of this paper, I shall have occasion to advert to the errors in argument and the delusions in opinion, as well as to the serious practical injury, which have arisen from the want of a clear understanding and a suitable appreciation of the *truth* I have stated.

II.

Such, then, having been the happy condition of those States at the inauguration of the rebellion and such having been the uniform paternal conduct of their Government toward them, I state another proposition which is self-evident, viz.: That for those blessings, as beneficent and as bounteous as were ever showered by the Almighty on any people, those States and their people were indebted to that Constitution and that Union for the overthrow of which the rebellion was commenced and is continued.

It is well known that the "Confederation" which was superseded by the Constitution of "'89" was a feeble and inefficient political structure, powerless alike for the purposes of internal government and of external relations. We did not become, for any available and permanent purpose, *a nation* till the adoption of the Constitution; all prior to that was incipient, imperfect and preparatory; by that wonderful work of genius, of wisdom and of foresight, we took our place among the nations of the earth; we became in a political and governmental sense the "American People." The people of those States became an integral part of that nation; they became the participators in its glory and power; they became entitled to the proud name of "American Citizen," and to the protection everywhere of the flag of their country; they lived, and prospered, and flourished solely under and by means of the Constitution and laws of that country; and, while in many and important particulars they were also citizens of States, in all that related to *nationality* they were citizens of "The United States of America." Their country was not their "State," it was "The United States; their *nation* was not the nation of South Carolina, of Georgia, of Texas, it was the "American Nation;" and by that title only they and we alike were known and recognized by the world.

This truth, like the other, must be kept continually in mind and must be solemnly pondered by all who investigate this great subject in the spirit of candor, integrity and patriotism, and with the honest desire to form a just judgment on a matter so momentous in all its aspects.

Under the facts above stated, the truth of which can never be disputed, it is absolutely impossible that the rebellion can for a moment be *justified*, or that it can in reality have had its origin on the ground that the Government of the country, either in its theo-

retical principles or the fundamental rules prescribed for its conduct or in its practical administration, has not fully answered its
great and beneficent purpose of securing to the people of those
States, in common with the people of the remainder of the Union,
all the blessings of every kind ever intended to be secured, or ever
in fact secured, by any government yet adopted by, or devised, for
man individually or as a member of a commonwealth.

III.

What, then, were the real causes, the actual originating motives,
of this scheme for the overthrow of such a government and the
destruction of such a nation? It is not difficult to ascertain nor so
to state them as to render them clear to all earnest seekers after
truth. The scheme is not of recent origin; it dates at least as far
back as the *first* term of the administration of President Jackson,
and its first open manifestation was in the attempt at nullification
then made by a portion of the people of South Carolina. It was at
that period, and before, evident to a few aspiring, ambitious men
of that and others of the States now in rebellion, that by the
more rapid progress of the States of the North in population,
material strength and every thing pertaining to national prosperity
and advancement, the time was not very far distant when the preponderating influence in the national Government and councils,
which had therefore been claimed by and conceded to those men and
their brethren and sympathizers, must in the ordinary and inevitable
course of events cease to exist or be very greatly diminished. It was
equally evident to those men that the operation of the *democratic
principle* of our Government would gradually sap and ultimately
undermine the foundations of the aristocracy to which they be-
longed, and which, to every essential purpose, entirely controlled
the population within their borders. We have only to look at the
facts of the census to convince us of this truth. Those States con-
tain, (in round numbers,) four hundred thousand slaveholders, four
and one half millions of non-slaveholders, (the vast majority of
whom are what is denominated there "poor whites," or "white
trash,") and three and a half millions of slaves. These numbers
are not precisely accurate, but sufficiently so for all practical purposes. It is an undoubted historical fact, which no candid man

will deny, that the political power and the social pre-eminence of
that whole country were possessed by the slaveholders. It required
no prophetic eye to foresee or to foretell, that the introduction there
of the ideas of the political equality of all *white* men, and the dig-
nity of labor, and of the truth of the sentiment in this regard announced in the "Declaration of Independence," would, if accom-
panied by education and consequent intelligence, gradually weaken
and ultimately and at no very remote period, destroy, the aristocracy which naturally was so dear to them. They could not but
see and realize that, between the millions of the subordinate white
race among them and the millions of men at the North, who in
different modes "earned their bread by the sweat of their brow,"
there must of necessity arise in time a strong bond of sympathy;
and that, whenever the real state of things came to be understood
and appreciated by that class of their people, they would assert
their manhood, and claim the same position politically and socially enjoyed by men of the same class in other sections of the
Union.

There is the highest authority for saying, that the leading and
influential men of the rebel Aristocracy dreaded the introduction
of the "democratic" principle among their people. One of them, in
1851, then holding an important office at the seat of the Government
of the nation, declared that "democracy is incompatible with the
whole system of Southern society." Another, in 1855, in speaking
of the democratic theory of Government by a majority, says, "it is
more powerful and more grinding in its tyranny than the Czar,"
"more infallible than the Pope," and "that in England the ability
to govern has been preserved by a highly *aristocratic* constitution,
both social and *political*." Another, in 1861, declares that the
"Union has served its purposes; at the North the progress and
tendency of opinion is to democracy; the South must so modify
its institutions as to remove the people farther from the direct exercise of power; at the South men see the necessity of stronger
government, its people are the most aristocratic in the world, and
aristocracy is the only safeguard of liberty." Another eminent
Southern writer, in the same year, says, "those pestilent and per-
nicious dogmas, 'the greatest good to the greatest number,' 'the
majority shall rule,' are the fruitful source of disorders never to be
quieted, revolutions the most radical and sanguinary, philosophies
the most false, and passions the most wild and destructive. The

2

experiment of the democratic Republic of America has failed." The person now holding the second office in the rebel government, in giving in his adhesion at the commencement of the rebellion, declared as his reason for the step " the indispensable necessity of founding a *new government* based on the *social system of the South.*" Another of their leading men argued that " the Government should be taken from the 'heels of society' (meaning the many) and 'placed in the head' (meaning the favored few)." From the year 1830 to the inauguration of the rebellion, in public addresses, private letters, leading newspapers and favorite literary periodicals in those States, similar sentiments are found in such abundance that there can be no doubt of the prevailing, and it may be said, the uniform feeling and opinion in this particular of the "governing" class there. We thus have the two great operative causes and influencing motives of that "class," and more especially of its ambitious and aspiring members, which impelled them to undertake the destruction of the Union, viz., personal ambition and hatred of democracy. I have no hesitation in deliberately declaring these to have been the causes and the motives. The case and the truth cannot be better stated than in the *New York World* of October 4, 1862 :

" The Northern people have accepted this war on too narrow grounds altogether. They have comprehended but a very meagre portion of the real interest at stake—for the very good reason that they have hardly begun to understand the spirit and aims of the rebel leaders. Had there been a better appreciation of the actual truth, the war would never have lagged as it has been suffered to do from the beginning.

" The evidence of such men as Col. Hamilton, who is fresh from the active scenes of the rebellion, and who has watched it with penetrating eye from its first step, is of peculiar value. Their conclusions, formed on the spot, face to face with the monster, are of infinitely more weight than the notions of Northern men, who know it only by occasional glimpses in the far distance. It is well that their testimony should be brought before our public whenever it can be obtained. The gentlemen who have induced Col. Hamilton to address our people with instruction and appeal, have done the good cause precious service. . . . . Col. Hamilton has no hesitation in pronouncing the issue now pending to be THE VERY HIGHEST, AND BROADEST, AND DEEPEST possible. It is, to his mind, nothing more nor less than A STRUGGLE BETWEEN THE ULTIMATE PRINCIPLES OF CIVIL GOVERNMENT—a question whether *the rule of the few* or *the rule of the many* shall prevail. He presents it as his settled conviction that *the leaders* in this rebellion are actuated by a distinct purpose to SUPPLANT POPULAR GOVERNMENT and ESTABLISH A MONARCHY, and that this comes from their belief that *slavery can have no effectual safeguard except what the strongest form of government can afford.* Therefore, he warns us not to rest upon the idea that mere territory, or even mere nationality, is at stake in this conflict. What has really got to be decided, as he justly views it, is, not whether the flag itself shall be deprived of a third of its stars, or whether the flag itself shall continue to exist, but *whether the Republican principle*, which has given the flag all its glory, *is or is not to perish*. He rightly declares that the co-existence of a Monarchy and a Republic between the Great Lakes and the Gulf, is a civil impossibility—that such an experiment would only be *another name for perpetual war*.

" We are, therefore, shut up to the absolute necessity of meeting this question now, once for all, and in fidelity to the great principles of the Declaration of Independence, which our forefathers sealed with their blood, are bound to prosecute this war with an energy and a self-devotion far beyond any thing we have yet displayed. These are great facts which Col. Hamilton seeks to enforce. He talks like a man who is thoroughly pervaded by a sense of their awful moment—and no mind that heeds his disclosures and his arguments, can doubt that he is right."

That the aspiring, determined and sleeplessly vigilant leaders of that " class" *actually had* the influence I have ascribed to them in inaugurating the rebellion, is demonstrated by the whole history of its commencement and progress, and is fully attested by the evidence of hundreds of the intelligent and enlightened Southern friends of the Union, among whom I may name Governor Hamilton of Texas, Lorenzo Sherwood, now of New York, but for fourteen years immediately preceding 1860, a resident of Galveston, Texas, and a distinguished lawyer and Democratic politician ; the eloquent Colonel Anderson, by birth a Kentuckian and by residence a Texan ; Andrew Johnson* and Judge Catron of Tennessee, John Minor Botts of Virginia, General Gantt of Arkansas, the lamented Pettigrew of South Carolina, Judge Wayne of Georgia, Governor Boorman of Western Virginia, the eminent and pious Dr. Breckinridge of Kentucky, Governor Pierpont of Eastern Virginia ; distinguished men in Missouri too numerous to mention, many of whose names are familiar to us all ; Clemens of Alabama, Bouligny of Louisiana, Blair of the District of Columbia, Davis of Maryland.† These persons, with one or two exceptions, were

* This gentleman, in a public address at Nashville on the 10th of June last, said : " This aristocracy has been the bane of the rebel States. One of the chief elements of the rebellion is the opposition of the slave aristocracy to being ruled by men who have risen from the ranks of the people. One of them, holding an important official position, said to me, ' We the people of the South will not consent to be governed by a man who has risen from the ranks of the common people.' This man uttered the *essential spirit and feeling* of the Southern rebellion."

† The Englishman Russell, the well known correspondent of the London *Times*, and who had no sympathy with the cause of the Union, visited South Carolina a few months after

natives of the South and slaveholders. The proofs on this point might be indefinitely multiplied. That those "leaders" *could have had* the influence ascribed to them, though a small minority of the voting population of those States, can easily be believed when we look at the social state of things, the prevalence of the fatal political heresy of " the right of secession," the prejudice against the North, the pervading ignorance, and the relentless despotism in reference to the liberty of speech and of the press in *one* particular, existing among that people in 1860 and for at least the whole preceding part of the present century.

The people of the States in which slavery is unknown, have but an inadequate idea of the aristocracy produced by that institution as it exists in the rebel States, and of the insidious but effective manner in which it subordinates the " many" to the " few." A brief residence there or a tour through those States would satisfy the most sceptical that the "governing" class, socially and politically, and for every practical purpose, is this aristocratic class, which, by long usage and common consent, occupies the position of conceded supremacy. Among this class there is again a natural division ; on the one side, those who by education, ambition, taste, family prestige, or otherwise are the " leaders" of their " class ;" on the other, the portion by far the most numerous, who pursue the " even tenor of their way," superintending their plantations and their slaves, seldom or never going beyond the bounds of their own States or (in many instances) even of their own immediate districts, having, as a general rule, but limited education and but little knowledge of the world or its doings outside of their own boundaries. I know that many will hardly credit this statement, but its truth will be testified to by any candid, intelligent and observing man who has had the opportunity of seeing the interior of that portion of the Union. On this point I refer with entire confidence to the volumes of Frederick Law Olmstead,* late General Secretary of the United States Sanitary Commission, the accuracy of whose statements in many particulars is known to me by personal observation. Thus, the very large bulk of the *slaveholding* population furnished an inviting field for the operations of those who placed themselves at the

their ordinance of secession, and was admitted to the confidence and social intimacy of her leading men. He states expressly in his published letters in the London *Times*, that those men often expressed to him their preference for a monarchical government and for aristocratic institutions, and made no disguise of their sentiments in this particular.

* " Seaboard Slave States," " Texas Journey," " A Journey in the Back Country."

head of the movement of rebellion. Then, as to the *non-slavehold-ing* class, no one can deny that, with the exception of a compara-tively small number engaged in mercantile and the higher branches of mechanical and manufacturing pursuits, that class is of a very low order, denominated in some of those States " crackers," and in all of them " white trash." This class, with the exceptions above mentioned, was for all practical purposes, so far as related to politi-cal matters, especially those concerning the peculiar social system of the rebel States, under the lead and control of the same "few" who led and guided the great proportion of their own slaveholding class. To this must be added the undeniable fact of the general want of education among the people of both classes, a want produc ing in the vast majority of them gross ignorance, and in a large proportion of even slaveowners themselves a degree of ignorance unknown among the bulk of the population of the " free" States of the Union. Then again the dogma of the " right of secession," and of the consequent supreme allegiance due to a State had been sedulously inculcated by their leading politicians and statesmen, almost from the organization of the National Government, cer-tainly from the beginning of the present century, so that it had be-come the creed of nearly all the people who had intelligence enough to form any opinion. It was a subtle poison, imbibed as it were, in early infancy, by a great majority of the present generation there. We see its practical fruits in the otherwise unaccountable desertion of their country's flag and violation of their solemn, repeated oaths by officers of the Army and Navy, and a similar violation by numerous incumbents of the highest civil stations ; and those very men, almost without exception, indebted solely to that country, " The United States of America," for all that distinguished them from the common mass of their fellow-citizens. So virulent was that poison, thus early imbibed, and so thoroughly permeating the whole head and heart of the individual man, that in many instances within the last four years, it has been seen to operate in those, who in early youth left their Southern birthplace, and had spent the last twenty or thirty years in happiness and pros-perity and honor among their brethren of the North. Yet they "owed their allegiance to the State of their birth," and HAVE ACTED ACCORDINGLY. Then, again, a bitter prejudice against the North has been unceasingly instilled into the minds of the whole population for a long series of years by ambitious and unscrupulous* men, so that in their condition of ignorance and seclusion, multitudes of them had come to believe us their natural enemies.

It is also to be remembered that, so far as their social system and every matter connected with it, nearly or remotely were concerned, there has literally been for more than half a century no liberty of speech or of the press within the rebel States. In no part of the globe has there existed in this respect a more relentless tyranny. The natural results followed; ill-will, prejudice, credulity, susceptibility of false impressions, blind infatuation. It is a well known fact, also, that the scheme of rebellion had been plotted by the leading conspirators long before its actual outbreak; and that, preceding that period, those conspirators and their associates had possessed themselves of, or placed it in their power to possess, to a great extent, the military material as well of the United States as of their several States. Accordingly, though at the very beginning of the attempt to force their States into actual separation from the Union, there was in many of them a majority of *votes* against it, yet in the state of things already shown to exist, and with the aid of the arms and munitions of war they had taken care to provide themselves with, it was no difficult task for the conspirators between the 21st of December, 1860, and the 1st of May, 1861, to bring about the results, which struck the nation and the world with amazement and horror.† The conspirators did their work entirely

---

* I make the following extract from an authentic statement recently published as to the condition of things in Texas. The description is precisely applicable to every rebel State: "Perhaps there was never a people more bewitched, beguiled and befooled, than we were when we drifted into this rebellion. We have been kept so to an amazing extent. Our editors, our preachers and stump-speakers, inflamed the people with falsehoods of rights violated, constitutions broken, laws disregarded, on the one hand, and easy victories on the other; and it is astonishing how easily the pretended secession was made and the war began. True, the people's ignorance made it an easy matter; but that does not excuse the persevering misrepresentations. Statements like this (by one since an officer of high rank) were common: 'I will give a good bond to drink all the blood shed in a war caused by secession.'"

† Mr. James Brooks, now Member of Congress from New York, traveled extensively in the rebel States some years since, and published an account of his observations and experiences. In relating a conversation he had in South Carolina with one of the non-slaveholding class, who could read and was intelligent beyond his fellows, he says: "This conversation gave us a good idea of the feelings which have wrought up the mass of the people in South Carolina to such an exasperation. This man is by no means a specimen of the intelligent nullifiers, but he is a good specimen of the backwoodsmen *who were to do the fighting.* The high-mettled fellow had been first taught to ' damn the Yankees;' next, to cultivate an undue State pride; then to believe his State was omnipotent, and her continuance in the Union all important, and indispensably necessary to support the Government. He solemnly believed, and would have taken his oath, that South Carolina paid all the taxes of this vast

through *conventions;* in no State was a majority of the votes of the *people* ever given for separation.* I have adverted thus briefly to these matters, for the purpose of presenting a conclusive answer to the wicked and mischievous fallacy which has occasionally been put forth among us, that the rebellion was the deliberate, well-considered, solemn, voluntary, earnest act of the *people* of the rebel States, and not induced by the machinations or the wiles of ambitious and unprincipled leaders, determined on the overthrow of democratic republican institutions and the substitution of a governmental system, under which the *laboring* classes, *black and white,* would be alike and for ever subordinate. Had the rebellion been in truth, as has been so falsely alleged, the deliberate act of that people, it would doubtless have been entitled from us and from the world to more respect and more lenient consideration ; but even in that case, it would have resulted from motives and causes so wholly erroneous, delusive, and unfounded, and its practical consequences, if successful, would have been equally so ruinous and fatal to the country, that our imperative duty would then have been, as it is now, at all hazards to defeat and overthrow it, and thus *to save our nationality.* In thus affirming the GENERAL condition of the people

Union. At a hundred million of dollars he set down her burthen! A *foreign* nation was about to subdue him and his State, and his pride rose on the reflection, and he was ready to throw his life away in attacking a fortified castle on an open raft! *Mr. Calhoun's well-instructed backwoodsmen of whom he boasted in Congress, are as ignorant of the extent, power and complicated interests of this Government as are the Rocky Mountain Indians."* He fully confirms all I have said as to the *non-slaveholding class.* He also equally confirms all my statements as to the ignorance, delusion and prejudice of that class of *slaveholders,* to whom I attribute those qualities. If he would now republish what he then wrote, all which was then true and is now true, he would render a valuable service to his countrymen.

* Two works recently published, "Loyalty on the Border, etc.," by Col. Baker, 1st Ark. Cavalry, and "Scenes in the War in Arkansas, etc.," by Wm. Baxter, perfectly illustrate the mode in which every rebel State, with two or three exceptions, was led into the rebellion. These writers tell us: "In the first convention which met in Arkansas the secession ordinance brought up by the conspirators was voted down by a majority of over two-thirds. This ought to have been conclusive. The excitement had been great; the people's minds had been inflamed by artful misrepresentations; every effort had been made to get a majority to vote for secession, and finally, to persuade the more pliable Unionists not to vote, and thus let the conspirators carry their measure. But every effort failed; and with this decision, if they had meant honorably to submit to the will of the people, they would have rested. Did they? Not at all. They demanded an ordinance referring the question to the people—who had just decided by their vote in convention—and then led the Unionists into consenting to an adjournment subject to the call of the president, with the promise that he should not call the convention together till after the people had voted in August. But the president of the convention, who had procured his election on the pretense of being a Union man, was one of the conspirators : he called the body to meet on the 6th of May. Sumter had just fallen, and the country was in a blaze of excitement; this was a good opportunity for the traitors. They collected an excited crowd in the hall where the

of the rebel States in reference to education, intelligence, and prejudice, it is by no means asserted that there were not many of whom that condition could not be predicated. Nor is it to be asserted, that there were not and are not among that people some, whose devotion to their country has continued an operative principle in the midst of the dangers and difficulties that environed

convention met, and no sooner had the roll been read than a member arose, presented an ordinance of secession, and moved that the yeas and nays be taken on it without debate. Under the manipulation of the traitor Walker, the presiding officer, this was done. Every 'aye' was received with a thundering shout from the infuriated crowd; the 'nays' were given in silence. Then Walker arose, and amidst jeers and threats against Union men, urged the 'noes' to recant, and, frightened and discouraged, all did so but one. His name was Murphy; he was compelled to fly from the State; he is now its loyal Governor. Thus by a series of frauds the conspirators attained their end. First by the help of the Knights of the Golden Circle a legislature was elected, which called a State convention. That convention, chosen hurriedly, without giving the people time for consideration, in the midst of wild excitement, yet refused to do the bidding of those who had procured its call. Rebelling against its decision, which they had engaged to hold final, they now demanded the submission of a secession ordinance directly to the people. The Unionists, conscious of their strength, consented to this also, and were cheated into adjourning the convention until the popular vote should be taken. Then once more the conspirators broke the agreement, and refused to wait for the verdict of the people which they had themselves demanded. They called the convention and pushed through their measures by violence. That is the way a *coup d'état* is effected in a Republic. But, the reader will say, if the Union men were in a majority, why did they submit? They submitted, because their enemies at once began to murder, imprison, rob, and exile them; because the secessionists had arms in their hands, and pursued, with bitter cruelty, every Union man who dared utter his sentiments; because 'seventy-seven loyal men were chained together, two and two, with an ordinary log chain fastened to the neck of each,' and thus marched for six days through the country to Little Rock, where they were offered the alternative of 'volunteering' into the rebel army, or being starved in prison; because—so popular was the rebel service even in the beginning—one General offered for the capture of a Union man, Withite, 'living or dead,' 'seven thousand dollars and three honorable discharges from the Confederate service.' The Governor of the State was one of the leading conspirators; the president of the convention, as we have seen, was also in their councils at the time when he was elected by Union votes; the arsenal was in their hands; and no sooner was the ordinance of secession passed than Texas and Louisiana troops were sent into Arkansas to maintain the power of the secessionists, while the Arkansas regiments, as fast as raised, were sent across the Mississippi. That is the way Arkansas was made unanimous. Moreover, to be silent in those days was held a crime. Loyal men dared not speak their sentiments, nor dared they keep their mouths shut. Everywhere troops of other States were encouraged to perpetrate the most brutal outrages upon those who were suspected of loyalty. The mails were stopped, false news of Union defeats was industriously circulated. Washington was captured at least once every ten days, and the Union army routed continually. Fort Donelson was asserted to have been a glorious victory for the rebels, with thousands of prisoners; and while the weak minded were thus affected, the lives and property of those who still obstinately remained faithful were given over to the lawless Texans and Louisianians, who actually sacked Fayetteville, where they were quartered, and which is a part of the State which had declared almost unanimously for the Union. Elder Graham, a noble Kentuckian, who had removed to Arkansas to found the Arkansas College, whose life was devoted to the spread of education in the Southwest, was a Union man, and was forced to fly from the State—or be murdered. This is the nature of the 'great popular uprising in the South.' "

them. That faithful band will never be forgotten by a grateful country. These Unionists of the South and the rebels, the liberalists and the aristocrats of Europe, all agree in the character of the issue now on trial before the world. They all know and assent, that this war is, in fact, a struggle of the slave aristocracy of America, aided, encouraged, and sympathized in by the aristocracy of Europe on the one side, against democratic institutions on the other; or, as it has been tersely called by an able writer, "Slavery and Nobility vs. Democracy." Almost the entire body of the English nobility openly, and many of them actively, favor the rebellion; they know and they feel that its originators comprise in this country a distinct class, a class as clearly separated from the great body of the people in the rebel States as they themselves are from the masses in England. This, on the ordinary principles of human nature, and from the ineradicable feeling of "caste," leads to a cordial personal sympathy on their part with their "brethren" here. But, besides, and more emphatically, the aristocratic classes of Great Britain and of all Europe are sensitively alive to the fact, stated a few months since in the *London Review*, "that any one who knows what lies beneath the surface of European society, must be aware that the spirit of republican liberty is a snake that has been scotched, not killed." Those classes, in their moments of calm reflection, cannot but be tremulously apprehensive of the silent but continued "working" of the "leaven" of the French and American Revolutions. They cannot shut their eyes to the progress of liberal principles in England and on the Continent; they know that our great American Republic has ever had the enthusiastic admiration of multitudes of poets, orators, statesmen, and heroes in every country, and that it has at this moment vast numbers of earnest friends in all parts of Europe, especially in Great Britain; they know its absolute antagonism to their system, and that it is a living, glaring rebuke of those systems. Knowing all this, they know and feel that the overthrow of this Republic, arising as it did, under the most propitious circumstances, and successful as it has thus far been in its career, would be the most perfect and conclusive argument against the *possibility* of the existence of free institutions any where, and would tend directly and certainly to the perpetuation of their monarchical and aristocratical systems. So we find that the crowned heads of Europe (with a solitary exception,) and her nobility and aristocracy, almost universally, from their inmost hearts desire the success of this rebellion, and the consequent dismemberment and destruction of this Republic. Well, indeed, may *they* have these sympathies and these desires; for, without question, the wave that engulfs our institutions will roll back the tide of political liberty for generations, if not for centuries; and the light of the flames which consume our beautiful American edifice, will illumine the pathway of despots, monarchs, and aristocrats, and furnish them "a pillar of fire by day and of cloud by night," long after the present and many future generations shall have passed away.

There is no fancy in these statements; they are sober, solemn, *suggestive fact.*

Thus it is seen that "slavery" is the cause of the rebellion only because, by its intrinsic nature and character, it created in the rebel States a "distinction of class" and subordinated the millions of *white non-slaveholders* to the thousands of *white slaveholders,* and thus produced an aristocracy necessarily arrogant, ambitious, jealous of interference or encroachment, and determined to perpetuate its privileges and its powers by the continued subordination alike of the colored and the white.

This, they clearly saw, could be accomplished only by means of a political structure, whose "corner-stone," as declared by their Vice-President Stephens, was "slavery;" and with prophetic eye they discovered that such a structure could not be erected and maintained within the temple of the Union, because that sheltered and protected vast and increasing multitudes of *white* men, who would sympathize with *their* non-slaveholding whites, and gradually, though certainly, infuse into them ideas of political equality and social elevation. They saw the tremendous strides of the non-slaveholding States in population and in moral, intellectual and material advancement under the influence of an antagonistic system of labor; and in that they saw, or thought they saw, the downfall of their own social system. They saw that they had but one remedy, viz.: the destruction of that temple of Union and the erection outside of it, or on its ruins, of their own edifice. The aristocracy of the rebel States could not much longer, as they believed, flourish and preponderate in the Union; *the Union must therefore* DIE. All its glories, its prestige, its hallowed associations, the beautiful and magnificent promises of its future, must be buried without the hope of resurrection in the grave they were preparing for it. They *did not*, for they *could not*, make any complaint of any injustice, oppression, neglect, on the part of the Government of the Union; for under it they had enjoyed, as already stated, unvaried prosperity and security; they could not, with the least pretense of truth, assert any fear of an adverse change hereafter in the principles and measures of the Government; but they *could* assert that communities living under a system of compensated labor and in which all white men enjoyed the blessings of education and the consequent power of self-elevation, outstripped them in a marvellous degree in all the constituent elements of national prosperity and advancement. They saw, too, as one of their most eminent citizens stated in my hearing in Georgia a quarter of a century since, that the "spirit of the age" was adverse to their peculiar system. Seeing all this, they could not but see that the only chance for the protection of that system, and of the "superior class" born of it, was in the establishment of an independent empire of their own. They did not probably see that such an empire might not endure for ever, but this was not material. Thus, incidentally and thus only, did "slavery" become a cause of the rebellion.

On the other hand, "abolition" was equally innocent of being its originating cause. Its only share in the matter was, that it furnished the *leading conspirators* with a war cry, a shibboleth, to address to the fears, the passions and the prejudices of the less enlightened of their own class, and with which to operate effectively on the ignorant and deluded masses of the subordinate class. How influentially they used it, the result mournfully shows. No man who watched the proceedings day by day of the Charleston Convention of June, 1860, and the subsequent acts of the prominent leaders of the rebellion, will hesitate for a moment to say that the real operative motives of those men, in preventing a nomination there, was to distract and divide the great Democratic party, to render it impossible for them to unite on a Presidential candidate, and *thereby to insure the election* of the candidate (Lincoln) already nominated by the Republican party; and that object being accomplished, to "fire the Southern heart" by the announcement, in every mode that ingenious falsehood could devise, that Abolitionism had triumphed, an Abolitionist had been elected President; that the scenes of St. Domingo would speedily be re-enacted throughout the rebel States, unless they protected themselves by forming a separate and independent government, and that now was the time for *revolution*. The state of things existing in that region (as already described), as to popular prejudice, ignorance, delusion and credulity, provided a ready and a willing recipient of those impassioned appeals. In popular meetings, in private assemblages, in State Conventions, in the newspapers and magazines, indeed, in every possible mode, after the meeting of the Electoral Colleges in December, 1860, and in fact as soon as the result of the election in the Fall of that year was known, the people of the rebel States were urged by these incessant appeals of the most inflammatory character to rise in insurrection against their Government, and, in the language of their leaders, " to throw off the hated yoke of abolitionism." And too well did those leaders succeed ; for within five months eleven of those States were induced (without, however, as I have already stated, *a popular vote*,) to join in the rebellion. The fact cannot be denied that, had the Charleston Convention with unanimity and cordiality nominated a candidate, the Democratic party would have triumphed, that candidate would have been elected, and the spirit of rebellion would have slumbered at least for a while. But no event could have been more undesirable to the rebel conspirators, for then they could not have raised the war cry of abolition, and their overt acts of treason must have been postponed for a season. Were these undeniable facts fully understood and appreciated among us, it would seem impossible that any man, especially any man of the Democratic party, who voted as I did in November, 1860, for the anti-Republican electoral ticket, could, even if uninfluenced by patriotic considerations, look upon the rebellion and its authors with any other feeling than that of deep indignation and absolute loathing, *for the reason* that with cruel deliberation and for an infamous purpose they distracted, divided and defeated that party in that great national election.

I have thus briefly but truly stated the secret and real motives and the actual causes of the rebellion, and without any fear that the impartial historian of this eventful time will present a different picture. The annals of the world afford no instance of an attempt, so wholly and absolutely without meritorious cause and so entirely without justification or even extenuation, to overthrow an established Government.

IV.

This being so, we must consider and endeavor fully to realize the direct and necessary consequences of the rebellion, if successful. The more calmly and deliberately such an inquiry is pursued, the stronger will be the conviction of the momentous interests involved in this struggle and the more brightly will the fire of patriotism burn in our hearts.

This rebellion has often with truth been said to be a rebellion against the " best Government on earth ;" that it is wholly without reasonable or even plausible cause is a fact established by the history of its origin, as has already been stated; it consequently, in a moral point of view, is a *crime* of unspeakable magnitude. It is in essence the work of a comparatively small number of men, incited to action by unhallowed ambition and by an earnest hatred of democratic institutions, and to whom an extraordinary opportunity for iniating their work was afforded by the social system existing in those States, and by the condition of the great masses of their population in the particulars which have been referred to. In the moral aspects of the case it may well be questioned whether those masses are chargeable with its iniquity. They, of course, are responsible in a legal sense for their acts; but acting, as they have and do, under gross error, delusion, and misrepresentation, and yet, as we are led to believe, in the belief of the justice of their cause, they stand in the eye of Omniscience and of the world in a moral position entirely different from that of those by whom they have been induced into their present course. And in speaking of the *crime* of this rebellion, the difference in this (the moral) aspect between the *leading conspirators* and the *body of the people* of the rebel States should never be forgotten. The former are to be *execrated*, the latter to be *pitied ;* and though the practical effects of wickedness of the one and of the delusion of the other, combined in action as they are, are the same, yet we should never lose sight of the *moral distinction.* The rebellion, under all its circumstances and in all its antecedents and concomitants, may well be termed the most heinous offense against God and against humanity, of which history furnishes any record. Its authors must at some time receive the reward due to those, who, to all moral intents, are guilty of the murder of the hundreds of thousands of their fellow beings, who, on the one side and on the other, have fallen in this conflict. That they, *the conspirators*, have sinned against light and reason and knowledge, no one can doubt, who knows the manifold opportunities they had, from their superior education and from long association with their fellow-citizens of the non-slaveholding States, of knowing *for a certainty*, that the appeals they made to the people of the rebel States and which led those States into the rebellion—appeals in reference to the dark and wicked designs of the Government of the country, and of the people of the North, on the safety, prosperity, and honor of the people of their portion of the Union, *were absolutely and unqualifiedly false*. *They* plunged a nation enjoying all the manifold blessings of peace into war, a war of all others the most dreadful; a war between brethren of the same family; a war that has reduced their own then flourishing and beautiful region into an almost universal waste; that has already cost over half a million of human lives; has shrouded thousands of families in mourning, and excited the fears and anxious apprehensions of the lovers of civil liberty and free institutions throughout the world. This is *their* crime!! Can its enormity be exaggerated? But this does not embrace the whole, nor even the worst, in this catalogue of horrors. The object and ultimate design of the rebellion furnish the top-stone in this column of iniquity; for that object and design were to *dissolve the Union of these States;* to dismember our Country, to destroy our Nationality, and to erect out of a part of the broken ruin a sovereign independent State. These were the design and object, and, if accomplished, such would be the result. The success of the rebellion, and the consequent separation of the rebel States, and their recognition as a distinct and sovereign people would, *ipso facto*, work the entire subversion of the Union and send back the remaining States to their original condition as separate States. Instead of being parts of one great and united people, instead of being the constituent members of a *nation*, each State would thereby and contemporaneously become a distinct commonwealth, independent of every other State, and, in a political sense, would be in the condition of the provinces that composed the distracted and unfortunate Republic of Mexico. The Constitution would not in any sense remain the constitution of the States not in rebellion; it would instantaneously, with the recognized release of the rebel States from its obligations, equally cease to be obligatory on the other States; for it was not adopted as, and never was, the

Constitution of those latter States as a body and a people, but of the *whole* " *United States.*"

Thus, by the success of the rebellion, two results would inevitably follow: First, the departure of the rebel States from the political structure existing by means of the Constitution and the Union; second, the contemporaneous overthrow of that structure as to all the States not in rebellion, and the strewing over them its shattered fragments. This idea is one of solemn import, and has been but very little considered, and not at all *estimated,* by us of this portion of the Union; it adds tenfold to the gravity of the crime of the rebellion, and is enough to make any reflecting citizen shrink in dread from the view. Who has an imagination sufficiently vivid to picture the condition of the remaining States in this contingency?

It has often been thoughtlessly said by well-meaning people, "Why not let the rebel States go? why not let them depart in peace?" Little do such people comprehend the tremendous import, the real nature and the utter impracticability of such a sentiment. They do not reflect that there is no existing power under the Constitution of their country to carry out the idea. Neither house of Congress by itself, nor both houses combined, nor the President with or without them singly or jointly, have the slightest ability to authorize or consent to the separation of any one or more States from the Union; and, were that step as beneficent as it is in fact destructive, it could by no possibility be taken under the Constitution *as it is.* The continuance in the Union of the States originally composing it, or since constitutionally admitted into it, is as vital to our existence as a "nation," as air and food are to the physical existence of individual man. This is the fundamental, integral principle of our national vitality; destroy it, and our national life is gone. In the language of an eloquent writer, "The Constitution of the United States was the means by which republican liberty was saved from the consequences of impending anarchy; it secured that liberty to posterity, and left it to *depend* on their *fidelity to* THE UNION." "It made the people of those *several* States *one nation,* and gave them a standing among the nations of the world." "It is the prominent and all-important cause of our prosperity, and is the *great code of civil government* wrought by the fathers of our Republic."*

* Curtis' Hist. Const., Prf. xi, xiv.

" The *preservation of the Union* of the States is essential to the *continuance of their independence* and the continuance of republican, constitutional liberty." *

The " Madison Papers " abound in evidence that UNION is the distinctive, essential, *indispensable*, living element of our *nationality*. †

With the ten States now in rebellion, thus being part and parcel of its very essence and substance, stricken from it, it is no longer the *Union* formed by the *Constitution ;* it is no longer the *nation* of the " United States of America ;" it ceases to be that people known and spoken of by all other people as the "American People." This results necessarily from the very framework of our Government; the preamble itself to the Constitution declares that it " establishes this Constitution for the *United States* of America," the States originally united as well as those that subsequently, according to the Constitution, became united ; it is not, and from its very terms it cannot be, the Constitution of ten or twenty or any number of States less than the whole ; for the moment that it ceases to be the Constitution for the *whole*, it from the very necessity and nature of the case ceases to be the Constitution of any. In this statement of the matter there is nothing exaggerated or fanciful ; it is the statement of the simple truth, as will be conceded by all who understand the theory of our Government. Is it asked then, " is there no mode whereby it is possible to destroy this Union and disunite these States?" The answer is emphatically No, except by the annihilation of the Constitution and the consequent *termination* of our *national existence*. By whatever means the Constitution is annihilated and overthrown, contemporaneously with that event, *ipso facto, eo instanti*, occurs our *death as a nation* and the instant return of each State to its original condition of separate sovereignty and independence. Then legitimately ensue anarchy, confusion, *Mexican provincialism*, no *national* name, no standing among the nations of the world, no power or capacity *as a people* to assert rights or prevent or redress wrongs, " *rudis, indigestaque moles ;*" the contempt and derision of Christendom ! It is asked, could that state of things be remedied ? This question no human being can answer. The Almighty only knows. The answer depends on a great variety of complicated considerations, the effect of diversities of opinion ; col-

* Curtis' Hist. Const., Vol. II, pp. 10, 75, 136-7 ; Vol. I, 487-8.
† " The Madison Papers," 3 Vols. Washington, 1840.

lisions of personal and local interests; schemes of individual ambition; moral, political and social theories; the possible influences of
suspicion, jealousy and envy ; restless desires for "some new thing;"
love of excitement and untried experiment; and numerous other
matters arising out of the peculiarities of our geographical position,
the imperfections of humanity and the "ideas" of this "progressive
age." It may, therefore, well be believed, that it is not given to
man to see with any clearness into the future of such a state of
things. Who can tell, even if it be conceded that the ten rebel
States would, in the event of the dissolution of the Union, become
united States, whether all, or if not all, how many, of the remaining twenty-five States would become States *united* under one constitution and government and thus become a *nation?* No one will
have the hardihood to assert *as a certainty,* that five, or ten, or
twenty, or the whole twenty-five, or even any two of those remaining States would thus *re-unite.* It *may be* that *all* would; but what
power less than Omniscience can authoritatively so declare? and
even if such should be the *final* result, what in the mean time is to
be our condition? and what perils and exposures are we to encounter in the period intermediate the destruction of one government and the establishment of another, the death of one nation and
the birth of a new one! It is, undoubtedly, a prevailing idea among
us (the result wholly of a want of due consideration), that the rebel
States *can* be recognized by the States not in rebellion, as an independent people; and then, that the last mentioned States are still
"The United States of America" under the present Constitution.
It has been shown, I trust, that this is an error as manifest as it is
perilous.

But, even if the effect of the success of the rebellion would not, in
a constitutional and legal sense, be as I have stated, *practically* the
consequences of the recognition of the independence of the rebel
confederacy would be the same; the *precedent* is made, ten States
leave the Union—any other ten or one or twenty can, *on the same
principle,* do the same; the right to secede at will and without
cause is established ; the Union is a *rope of sand* and we are no
longer a *nation.*

The name of "American citizen" has been for eighty years a
proud appellation. By a singular, but for us, beautiful accident,
if I may so call it, the title of "American" is by the common consent of the world, Europe, Asia, Africa, and this Western Continent,

exclusively given to the citizens of "The United States;" and when "American," or "American citizen" is any where spoken of, it designates only a citizen of this Republic. There are Mexicans, Granadians, Peruvians, Brazilians, Chilians—but no "Americans" but ourselves. It is under this name that we are known and have been honored everywhere; it is the "American" flag that floats in power and beauty on every ocean; it is the "American" Republic that is the Eldorado of all, who long for political freedom; the "promised land" of multitudes of the suffering and the oppressed of other countries; the asylum now of millions, and the future asylum of many more millions of our fellow-men, attracted to it by the most persuasive and the most fascinating considerations.

But all this, our own great blessings and the hope and joy and stay of such multitudes elsewhere are but as "dust in the balance" in the view of the heartless conspirators of the rebellion, and are to be swept away for ever to gratify their personal ambition and their antipathy to the institutions founded by the common efforts and sacrifices of their and our fathers. The picture of the unexampled distress, desolation and misery already caused by the rebellion, cannot be overdrawn; its horrors, so long as this war continues, will equal or surpass those already witnessed; and should it—through the curse of God—prove successful, the page which records that success and its effects for generations to come on the great cause of civil and religious liberty, will be the gloomiest, the most frightful in all history. When we know, as we do, the absolute causelessness of the rebellion; when we look at the awful mass of human misery it has already produced and is still to produce, and when we consider its direful effects, if successful, on the highest and most hallowed interests of humanity, we involuntarily stand aghast at the spectacle. And while we weep tears of sorrow over the infatuation and delusion of the unfortunate masses in the rebel States, who have been deceived and persuaded into a participation in this awful work, we are at a loss to characterize the enormity of the *guilt* of the chief criminals.

By the great blessing of Almighty God, in induing with almost superhuman wisdom the Constitutional Convention of 1787, the "American" people have a Constitution whose perfect fitness for their national purposes has been fully proved by experience. It has been found to be in all respects adequate to the safe and happy government of the whole of our present imperial territory and population; and as adequate to the government of that territory and that population and any future increase of the latter, as it was for the government of the limited territory of the thirteen original States and their three millions of inhabitants. It is this blessed Constitution, which the rebellion is designed to overthrow; and thus to involve this favored land in anarchy, confusion, and dread uncertainty!!

The vast body of the people of the States not in rebellion, by whatever party name they may be called, love our institutions and the Constitution which originated and preserves them; not one in ten thousand sympathizes in this respect with the rebel aristocracy. Occasionally indeed such an anomaly is found among us. Since the commencement of the rebellion, I have seen one professed member of the Republican and one of the Democratic party, who each said, that he was indifferent to the result of this war; and when asked the reason, answered, that he did not consider man capable of self-government, and therefore did not desire the perpetuity of our institutions. But such sentiments are so rare here as to be of no practical moment. I will, before I conclude this paper, explain the apparently unaccountable course of many among us in reference to the rebellion—unaccountable, if we believe, as I do, that those very men, with a few exceptions, are sincerely attached to our institutions, are at heart patriotic and not justly obnoxious to the charge of disloyalty to their country.

I have thus, within the limits which the occasion demands, but by no means with the fullness which the unspeakable importance of the subject requires, stated the causes and motives of the rebellion, its objects and designs and its consequences, if successful. The picture is full of horror—but it is the horror of naked, unvarnished truth.

V.

Can a scheme so fraught with iniquity and evil succeed? From my inmost heart I rejoice to say, that its success is *impossible*. I believe in a God of Justice, of Truth, of Mercy and of Love. So believing, I cannot believe that He will permit the final triumph of a scheme, whose whole origin nature and object are at variance with each and every of those His attributes; I cannot believe, that He will regard with favor and crown with success a most stupendous crime against heaven and earth.   I cannot believe that He will permit the destruction of a nation which He has thus far signally blessed, and which to all human view He has raised up as a great palladium of civil and religious liberty; a nation distinguished from all others by institutions the best fitted to enable His creature man, *to be a man;* a nation so situated, territorially and geographically, and by the character of its institutions, as to justify in the enlightened philanthropist the brightest hopes of her effective instrumentality in the final civilization and Christianization of those races of the world which are now in darkness.

He has deeply afflicted and distressed the nation.   This affliction and distress may for a time be continued, but we may be permitted to believe, that all this comes as a punishment for national and individual sins and is intended to bring us back to a higher and a better, a more vivid and realizing sense of the favors we have received; that it is designed for our purification and improvement and to prepare us the better to act our great part on the theatre of the world; that in His own "appointed time and season," He will cause these sufferings to cease and will restore us individually and nation ally to our former condition of unity and concord, bettered in every high sense by our trials.

To this faith in the righteousness of our cause and the consequent favor and protection it will receive from the Great Disposer of events, we are enabled to add existing facts, furnishing as I conceive, sure grounds for the unqualified assertion, that this rebellion must at no remote period come to a close, disastrous and ignominious to its authors and abettors, and grateful and satisfactory to all patriotic men among us and to all elsewhere who love and cherish our institutions of " Republican liberty."

The actual commencement of the *war* of the rebellion was in April, 1861.   At that time the population of the States now in rebellion exclusive of slaves, was less than five millions, and of the remaining States, about twenty-four millions; the aggregate wealth and material power and resources of the former as compared with the latter, were in about the same proportion.   This statement alone would seem to render it absolutely certain that, in a conflict between the two parties with such an overwhelming preponderance of population and material power on the one side, the latter must ultimately triumph.   To hold the contrary would be to contradict all human experience and to believe that weakness is superior to strength. The utmost that could be said would be, that the weaker might prolong the contest beyond the brief period that would, under such circumstances, seem probable; but to believe that the party so wholly inferior in physical power could ultimately be victorious, would seem to be the vagary of a disordered intellect. We are now in the fourth year of this war; and while we may well be astonished that the rebel confederacy has under all the circumstances been able even so long to maintain it, in looking to the *future* we must contrast their and our *now* existing means and resources with the means and resources of each as they existed at the beginning of the conflict.

(1.) I will barely allude, without particularizing, to the immense losses of territory sustained by them first, in the entire practical withdrawal from the confederacy, of Western Virginia, Tennessee, Missouri; second, in the failure to obtain the accession of the States of Maryland and Kentucky, of whose co-operation they had the strongest hopes and expectations in April, 1861; third, in the actual occupation by us of large portions of Mississippi, Arkansas, Louisiana, and of very important parts of Florida, Georgia, South Carolina, North Carolina and Alabama. Thus, in this particular, they are shorn in July, 1864, of a vast amount of strength and power they actually possessed or confidently calculated upon in April, 1861.

(2.) It would be useless, were it possible, to specify with accuracy the frightful losses of men and material sustained by them thus far in this contest; reliable and authentic statements show, that of their population capable of bearing arms, about one half million have already been lost to them by death, disease and desertion. It requires but a bare comparison of their number with the number of arms-bearing men in a population of twenty millions to discover how disastrous, not to say ruinous, such a loss must be.

(3.) It is well known that already the most relentless and universal conscription* throughout the rebel States has been resorted to to fill up the ranks of their army; few if any between 16 and 60 escape; throughout that whole region it is a well ascertained fact, that there are scarcely enough able-bodied white men left even to control and

---

* The following is an extract from a letter of an officer of our Army, dated "Near Atlanta, July 16, 1864:" "It is but little Northern people know of the terrible and grinding system of oppression that is exercised by the leaders of this rebellion over those who are within their influence. Thousands of men are forced into this rebel army against their will, and are compelled to fight us, while they would willingly be with us."

direct the labor of the slaves and to perform other duties, not military, but indispensable to the carrying on of the war.

In truth, as to this class of people, that region is in every practical sense depopulated. The effect of this upon their future is too evident to require comment.

(4.) It is the concurrent testimony of all our officers and men who have had the opportunity of personal observation, and of the statements of the public papers throughout the rebel States, (with extracts from which we are often furnished,) that there is, if not a universal, a very extensive want of most of the necessaries of life in a large proportion of their territory. It does not require prophetic vision to discover that this is an evil which, under their circumstances, *cannot* grow less. On the contrary, from the very nature and circumstances of the case, it must continually become more and more intolerable.

(5.) The pecuniary condition, both of the rebel government and of the people, is to the last degree desperate. Their public debt is worthless, their public credit wholly gone, and the currency so degraded that, according to recent advices from their "seat of government" and other places in that region, the prices of every necessary and comfort of life are truly frightful.* How long, in this financial condition, will it be in the power of that government to furnish *the indispensable munitions of war*, and the pay, clothing, and rations of their soldiers?

(6.) In extensive portions of many of the rebel States, as in Virginia, North Carolina, Mississippi, Louisiana, Arkansas, Texas, all the sufferings of war have been, and are now being experienced, at the very doors of the people; in all their other States to a greater or less extent, its evils and its distress have been brought directly to

---

* The following were the hotel prices at Staunton, in Virginia, in June last: "Board and room, per day, $20; fire in room, extra, per day, $3; supper, lodging and breakfast, $15; single meal, $6." On the 30th of April last, in an important Southern city, the following were the prices: "Butter, $5 per pound; lard, $4 00 to 4 50; flour, $225 to 250 per barrel; rice, $45 to 40 per hundred; meal, $7 per bushel; bacon, $4 per lb.; salt pork, do; fresh beef, $2 50 to 3 per lb.; fresh pork, $3 40 to $4; dried apples or peaches, $5 per pound; green peas, in shell, $2 50 per quart; strawberries, per quart, with stems, $5; a cabbage head, from $3 to 5; and all other things in the eating line in proportion. Tea, $65 per pound; coffee, $20. A very common dress coat, $250, and from that up to $1,000. A thin Summer coat, from $300 to $100; a shirt, $50; shoes, $25; calico, $12 per yard; a silk dress pattern, $600, which will buy one hundred and fifty pounds of pork, or six pairs of ladies' shoes. A quart of milk, one dollar; a cow which will give twelve quarts of milk, from $600 to $1,000; pigs, $25." The following extract from an Atalanta paper shows the prices at Richmond in July, 1864: "The Richmond hotels are now kept on the European plan, and

the homes of thousands.* The prevailing ignorance and delusion in those regions, as they rendered the masses an easy prey to the machinations and wiles of the arch-conspirators, so they operate to conceal from them the truth in relation to the fatal blow their cause has already received,† and tend to deaden them for the time to the wide-spread distress they see around them.

When will this ignorance and this stolid submission end? They cannot on any principle known to human nature long continue, and on the coming of the hour, when the eyes of those masses shall be opened to the dread realities surrounding them, to the desperateness of the rebellion and to the true and real causes which produced it, there will, we have every reason to believe, be witnessed on the part of the *people* of the rebel States an uprising against the authors of their calamities, the throwing off the iron yoke of despotism, and a clamorous, resistless demand to return to the protection of that Government under which they had known nothing but peace, tranquillity, and security. Beyond all question, the great bulk of that people have been sincere in the delusion, that they were contending for their homes, property, and civil rights; indeed, they have been more than sincere, they have been enthusiastic—and enthusi-

every article called for at the table adds to the 'bill of fare' in a double sense. The following is the schedule up to the latest dates: Bacon and salad, $6; roast beef, $5; beef steak, $6; beef steak and onions, $8; tenderloin, $7; mutton chops, $6; pork steak, $6; soup, $2; fried onions, $3; pure coffee, per cup, $5; mustard, $2; lettuce, $3; boiled ham, $7; ham and (2) eggs, $10; butter (small taste of), $3. A single meal for a gentleman and his friend, dining as *ante bellum*, costs not less than $100." Of course, all the above were in rebel currency.

* In illustration of this, I select from multitudes of similar published statements, the following from a recent reliable letter from Texas: " The entire male population, except boys and old men, are in the war. The ground is left untilled. Manufactures we never had. Our herds of cattle and sheep, once our food, with our horses, all our wealth, are driven off or lying dead on our prairies, breeding sickness among us. Civil law—we do not know what it means. Every man relies on his six-shooter, or lets his property go without complaint. Schools, preaching, churches, have all been abandoned. The taxes levied by statute would take the largest share of the property. We are now eating the remainder of our last year's corn, and in cases not a few the beef that dies from starvation, with no present prospect that we shall have even these long."

† The same writer last quoted, says: " During the war we have been invariably successful. We have beaten the United States armies in every battle everywhere. We have killed more men and taken more prisoners (according to the published reports) than there were inhabitants in the loyal States at the last census. We have taken and burnt Washington I don't know how many times. We have driven the Government to Philadelphia, New York, and Cincinnati, each in turn, and finally we took the President and Cabinet all prisoners. We have made successful invasions through the Western States, to and including Chicago. Gen. Lee, last Summer, took Gettysburg, Chambersburg, Harrisburg, Philadelphia, Baltimore and Washington, all in a single week. The man came on here in person who went with the army the whole distance, and staid two days after it entered Washington.

asm, whether in a good or in a bad cause, produces the same results of patient suffering, obstinate perseverance, bold and reckless personal courage; and all these qualities have those people exhibited in abundance.

The same enthusiasm and delusion led the Musselman under Mahomet to deeds of terrible daring in the wars with the " infidels :" they were taught to regard, and did regard the killing of a "Christian" as a sure passport to Paradise. So the Crusaders in the Middle Ages, under a similar influence, exhibited unexampled personal heroism in their struggles for the recovery of Jerusalem; sincerely believing, as they were taught to believe, that a participation in

Our most intelligent men believe all this. And those of us who doubted that an army could move so fast or far, were careful not to say it. England, France and Russia have recognized our independence, and promised us aid several times. Generally the intelligence was official, always certain. Our bonds—Confederate and State—were at a premium in Europe. Money was pressed upon our Government, all and more than it needed. Even in Wall street our Confederate bonds were worth more than the United States bonds. Our soldiers were well fed and clothed, and everywhere (except right here) contented and in the best courage. The slaves (except also here) were a unit, clinging to their masters, and resisting emancipation. Our paper currency was as good as gold all over the Confederacy, (except again right here.) Don't think I have exaggerated. This is the uniform unbroken testimony of our papers, and preachers, and our stump speakers. Add to this that the United States were just on the brink of ruin—their debt overwhelming—their currency worthless—the time of service of their soldiers out, and they could not be coaxed or forced into the ranks again—do draft could be enforced—their people very unanimous against the war—and the President only able to exist by the protection of body guards. Why then should we not be in good courage—why not finish up the work, and, in the cant phrase of the day, 'gain our liberties?' From having regular and reliable mails, we have none in one-half of the State, and only get a letter or newspaper by chance conveyance. This, with verbal rumors, is our only source of information. We know literally nothing of the world outside of us. We have a rumor of trouble in Europe, but of its cause and condition we are ignorant. Till we saw New York papers, we knew nothing of the movements in Arkansas or Louisiana, for the reconstruction of loyal State Government, nor of the Emancipation movement in Delaware, Maryland, Missouri, etc. Such things are not told here. In fact we have learned more from these papers, about affairs in the United States and abroad, than we have known before during the whole war. It took us more than two months last Summer to find out that Vicksburg was captured. Our papers stoutly denied it, even after the paroled soldiers came home. And to this hour we are told that no boat can pass up or down the river--that they are fired into and sunk. Our currency is useless ; it will buy nothing. And yet our papers and our patriots tell us, that to make any difference between a paper and a silver dollar, is a crime deserving of punishment or hanging." The following is an extract from the editorial in the leading newspaper in Texas, the *Houston Daily Telegraph*, of the 21st of March last: " The Confederate army has whipped the Yankees all out of Alabama, Mississippi and Florida. Gen. Lee is driving Gen. Meade into Washington City, and will soon have the city itself. In one month we shall have San Francisco and all California. Secretary Seward is sick, and gone home to die of chagrin. The President and Secretary Chase are so down-spirited as to be really pitiable objects. It is all the United States can do to keep our troops from overflowing the entire Free States. And they have given up the idea and the attempt to conquer us." Volumes might be filled with similar extracts from papers in every rebel State. And these monstrous falsehoods are believed by that people, and *on this belief they act*.

that holy work would insure them everlasting bliss in Heaven. The enthusiasm of these misguided men of the rebel States is, in character, identical with that of the followers of Mahomet in his day and of the Crusaders in theirs; but such a "passion" from its very nature cannot be enduring; and in the case now before us, we have no right to doubt, that ere long it will "burn out" and that reason will resume its sway; and then, that the rebellion will end through means of the very men by whom its authors have thus far been able to sustain it.

(7.) Irrespective wholly of all questions of "abolition" and of all "sympathy for the slave," can any intelligent observer doubt, that under existing circumstances, the enormous slave population of the rebel States is to them an element not only of weakness, but of the most alarming danger, nay, of certain ruin.* Conceding the degradation and stolidity of that race, the events of the last three years have shown that the distinction between slavery and freedom is understood by vast numbers, if not by the great majority of them; that they have sufficient *intelligence* to make that distinction and sufficient of *human nature* to prefer freedom to bondage. In every part of that land they have heard, in the private conversations of their masters, in public addresses, and in various other modes, that this war was a war for the "abolition of slavery," and however false the assertion, while it subserved the intended purpose of its authors in "firing the hearts" of the whites, it subserved at the same time the unintended purpose of "firing" in another way "the hearts of the blacks." That ideas of freedom are widely disseminated among that class is not to be disputed. Moreover, thousands of them have been employed by the rebels themselves in various kinds of military work, and in some instances, as is well known, in actual military service. According to authentic accounts, not far from one hundred thousand of the black race are now fighting as soldiers in the army of the Union; and from the best authority we learn, that they have in this capacity done no dishonor to the flag under which they go into battle. None but he who doggedly shuts his eyes to the truth can fail to see that the slave population of that region, *as slaves*, is demoralized; that, as an element of productive labor, it cannot long be relied on; that as

---

* Mr. Cobden in a recent letter to a friend in this country well says, that "It is the condition of the South *through the operation of the war on the African race*, that I have always regarded as the real source of *weakness and danger to the South.*"

soldiers in the cause which their masters have taught them is the cause of "Slavery," and against the cause which they have learned from the same masters is the cause of "Freedom," it is morally impossible that they can be availably used, whereas on every principle and motive of human conduct (and in this regard, debased as they may intellectually and morally be, they must at least be conceded to be *human beings*), as well as from actual recent experience, we are entirely justified in the belief that they are destined now and hereafter to be a "thorn" in the side of the rebel confederacy and materially to add to the number and the effective power of the armies of the Union.

Much more might be added to this catalogue of *facts*, going to show the insuperable difficulties under which the rebellion labors, and, under the influences of which at no remote period it must totter to its fall.

We will now take a brief view of the condition of things correlatively in the States, which sustain the Constitution and the Union.

The overwhelming superiority of these latter States at the inauguration of the rebellion, in all that constitutes material or physical strength, and the natural, and it may well be said, the inevitable result of such a state of things have already been mentioned. Has the relative position of the parties been changed to the disadvantage of these States up to this period? I have already stated several particulars proving that the progress of the rebel States has been, in every practical sense, eminently "backward;" and that even if there was with them at the dawn of this awful day any brightness, that brightness has disappeared.

I will now very succinctly show the contrast between our *present* condition and the *present* condition of the rebel States in the foregoing particulars; and demonstrate, that while their condition and their prospects are incomparably worse than at the commencement of the rebellion, ours are in every essential respect vastly improved.

(1.) Having spoken of the loss of territory and of States they had confidently relied on, it is merely necessary in marking the contrast to say, that our gain is in proportion to their loss; and when we see the magnitude of their loss, we, at the same time, see the corresponding magnitude of our gain.

(2.) While it may be granted (though it is believed to be by no means *the fact*) that our losses in men numerically and in materials

of war in quantity are not less than theirs, still, when it is an undeniable fact that our resources in these respects were at least five
times greater than theirs, so it follows, that practically the loss
they sustain, is in the same proportion greater than that suffered by
us—in other words, that while in those particulars they, from the
very necessity of the case, are at the point of exhaustion, we are
not essentially impaired in strength and are at this moment fully
able to meet all necessary additional demands upon us.

(3.) While in the rebel States the most relentless conscription
has done its sweeping and desolating work, no such step has been
adopted or suggested here; the moderate resort we have made to
the draft is a measure wholly different in character and result: the
latter calls for a very small proportion of the whole body of male
citizens between the ages of eighteen and forty-five, and enables
those, on whom the lot falls, if they have the means and the inclina-
tion, to relieve themselves by substitute; whereas the former, by its
despotic and ruthless operation, *compels* into the army all male citizens between the ages of sixteen and sixty-five. The one is the
mode of a paternal government, the other is the creature of a
frightful despotism. It has resulted, as already remarked, in the
depopulation of that region as to this class of its inhabitants,
while we are still left with our *millions* of men of that description.

(4.) In none of the States not in rebellion (except in some
comparatively small portions of the States of Tennessee, Missouri,
and Western Virginia,) is there the slightest want *of all* the neces
saries and comforts and even luxuries of life. No complaint of this
kind has been heard among us. The war has not, in this respect,
had any perceptible influence; it has not been felt.

(5.) While multitudes of individual citizens of the rebel States
have been reduced, by reason of the rebellion, from affluence to
poverty, and still greater numbers have suffered distressing pecuniary loss, such effects are scarcely known here; they form the exception to the rule. A small number have sustained serious
pecuniary injury, resulting almost entirely from the investment of
means directly or indirectly in private or public indebtedness in the
rebel States. Indeed, on the contrary, our citizens, as a general
rule, have been pecuniarily benefited by the war. No class among
us, mercantile, manufacturing, agricultural, or mechanical was
ever more prosperous. The same favorable contrast exists in the
financial condition of our Government. While the rebellion has

devolved on us the necessity of raising very large sums for its suppression, the confidence of all classes in the credit of the Government is such, that no difficulty has been experienced in obtaining
on its securities all that was required ; this has been obtained prin-
cipally from our own people in sums varying from fifty dollars to
millions.* This great debt is thus mainly distributed among thousands of our citizens in all the walks of life. At this moment, in
all our important financial centres, this debt commands a premium.
True, the necessarily vast increase of the currency for the time being has raised gold to an exorbitant price ; but this *artificial* value
will in due time and without, it is confidently believed, producing
material injury, disappear and every article, including gold, will
return to its true value. That the universal confidence now felt in
our public securities rests on a *real* basis, and that the Government
debt will be honorably and honestly paid, I shall show before I
close this paper.

(6.) I have mentioned the prevailing misery and distress throughout the rebel States, the desolation of many of the heretofore most
prosperous and happy portions of that region ; indeed, *in one word*,
the horrors of war experienced by them by *actual war in their
midst*. We are total strangers to this dreadful suffering. Traverse
all *our* States, visit town and country, nowhere will be discovered
any indication of our being engaged in war, much less a war whose
proportions have not been equaled in modern times. To all appearance, peace, tranquillity, security, everywhere prevail and as
the appearance is, so is the reality. We are strangers to the *practical* evils and distress of war. With an occasional slight exception, not a single one of our States has been the theatre of military
contest. True, tens of thousands of our citizens are enrolled in our
armies and are fighting, far from their firesides, the battles of the
Republic. Mournfully true, multitudes of these gallant men have
been offered up on the altar of their country ; great domestic affliction has resulted ; still, so far as the *general* effect is concerned,
it may be asserted with literal accuracy, that we are entire strangers to the terrific desolation which has been experienced in such
melancholy profusion in every rebel State.

(7.) After the experience furnished by upwards of three years of
war, theory and *a priori* reasoning as to the effect of slavery on the

---

* Over $10,000,000 of the loan offered in June last was taken, principally by our citizens,
at an average premium of over four per cent.

rebel cause, give place to fact and reality. That it is to that cause a source of weakness and to the cause of the Union a source of strength, is fully established. This proposition might well be stated in stronger terms; it might truly be said, that the servile population of the rebel States is, under existing circumstances, a most perilous, if not a fatal, ingredient in the cup they have mixed for themselves. And when that cup has been drained to its last bitter dregs, among the bitterest will be found the residuum of the institution of slavery.

Very much more might be said in reference to the effect of slavery on the rebel cause; but I have not intended in this paper to do more than present a brief outline of the material matters affecting the great question before us, and thus rather to suggest ideas than to furnish a full exhibition of facts and the various conclusions legitimately flowing from them. The comparison I have thus briefly instituted between the relative condition of the States in rebellion and of those not in rebellion, as that condition was at the inauguration of the rebellion and as it now is, must convince the most incredulous, that however sanguine the hopes and however bright the prospects of the rebels may have been at the beginning, the "stern logic" of now existing facts has destroyed all foundation for those hopes and has shrouded those prospects in the deepest gloom.

It may be emphatically stated, that the great body of the people of the States not in rebellion. irrespective of party, has solemnly and irreversibly resolved that their nationality shall not be destroyed; that the proud name of "American Citizen" shall not be obliterated; that their country shall not be disintegrated and converted into as many petty, warring, discordant, insignificant provinces as there are now States; that "Republican liberty" shall not perish; and having so resolved, they have by necessary consequence resolved, that the Union must and shall be preserved; and in order thereto, that the States in rebellion shall never—no, never—be recognized as a nation, and that the rebellion shall be wholly, absolutely and for ever crushed. That such is the fixed determination and stern resolution of the great bulk of our people is susceptible of clear demonstration.

VI.

The facts and considerations already presented show the impossibility of the success of the rebellion; its designs cannot be accomplished; those States cannot leave the Union and become an independent nation. The precise day of the final extinction of this scheme for national destruction cannot at this moment be stated; every thing indicates that it is not remote. In view of this certain result, the *status* of the several States and especially of the rebel States at its termination, becomes a question of unspeakable importance. Various theories have been advanced, and various plans suggested for what is termed "re-construction." In my judgment that term is entirely inapplicable and its use leads only to error and confusion. We cannot "re-construct" that which has not been destroyed; and the very first proposition, the fundamental idea, is that the Union not only *is not*, but cannot be, destroyed by the rebellion. What, then, is to be the condition of the rebel States at its overthrow and how are they then to be regarded and treated?

1. The answer to this question is not difficult, if we give due attention to two matters: first, to the fact, that underlies our very existence as a nation and which is inseparable from the very idea of our nationality, viz.: that the Union is not dissolved, but stands on the same firm and enduring basis on which it was originally erected; second, the great fundamental principle, *that the Constitution must be preserved sacredly inviolate in its every provision.* The absolutely vital importance of not infringing on or violating in any manner this fundamental charter, this very essence of our national life, is a proposition heartily adopted by every true American citizen. I cannot better state this matter than in the eloquent and forcible words of Count de Gasperin.* Knowing the desire expressed by some overzealous men that the President should proclaim "universal" emancipation, he says, "The independence of the States must be protected with jealous care." "I counsel no measure that would not be strictly constitutional. I should have grossly contradicted myself if, after having advised Americans to preserve their institutions and retain them at the end of the war as they were at its beginning, I had urged them to violate them in their fundamental principle. The *liberty of the* STATES is no less

---

* "America before Europe," pp. 562, 567, 568. His other great work, "The Uprising of a Great People," contains similar warnings.

important to be maintained than the *sovereignty of the nation.* A rebellion by the South *against the Constitution* should not be combatted by a *similar rebellion* by the North. The two original features of the American organization should neither perish in the furnace of civil war. It will be glorious to see the United States come out of it with their *local* independence and their *national* unity alike unimpaired."

This is the testimony of a distinguished and earnest friend of our country, and whose works have produced, and will long continue to produce, in Europe, the most benign influences in our behalf. He expresses this sentiment while, at the same time, he is a most ardent advocate of negro emancipation everywhere. I make this extract merely to show the sensitiveness on this subject of those eminent foreigners, who know and love us best; they realize, even more vividly than ourselves, any departure from the "great charter" of our liberties as fraught with inconceivable peril. Keeping in mind the *fact* and the *principle* just mentioned, the result necessarily follows, that the rebel States are, (as they have never in a legal and constitutional sense ceased to be,) members of the Union—component parts of the "American Nation," States of "the United States of America." But the people of those States are in rebellion against the Government, seeking to destroy the Union by the overthrow of the Constitution; and *while in this condition,* the performance of their duties and fulfillment of their obligations as members of the Union are by their own act prevented, and, in a constitutional sense, their State functions in that regard (that is, as members of the Union,) are in a condition of suspension. What, then, is the first, the indispensable step to be taken by the Government of the Nation? Obviously, it is to *crush the rebellion,* to end it *in toto.* To this result the entire destruction of the *military power* of those States is an indispensable preliminary. "Extermination," "subjugation," in reference to the *people* of those States, "extinction" of their State Governments *as State Governments,* are the words of fanaticism or of folly. Annihilation of their *military power* is the demand of wisdom, of patriotism, of duty to the Republic. And by military power I mean not only armies in the field, but all armed bodies small and large and everywhere. Without the accomplishment of this object, vain is all endeavor effectually to quell the rebellion and thus restore its wonted peace, tranquillity and security to our country.

The reason of the absolute necessity to this great end of this entire annihilation of that military power is obvious. If that continues even in a slight degree, even in the form of bands of guerrillas, no real security would exist for the complete ascendancy *of the law*, and for its thorough, absolute, and effective administration. Courts could not be held, their judgments could not be executed, if liable to interference from armed men, even in small numbers.

It is certain that there can be no real or available restoration of domestic tranquillity throughout our borders, no full restoration of the Union to the " *status in quo ante bellum*," no replacement of all its members under the ægis of the Constitution, until the period arrives when the judicial tribunals of our country can, in all respects, execute their functions as safely and as efficiently on the banks of the Alabama, the Chattahoochee, the Santee, the Pedee and the James, as they now do on the banks of the Hudson and the Delaware. And this period cannot come, so long as there is any more danger from *military violence of any sort* in the former than in the latter regions.

Let it not be said that the idea of such and so complete an annihilation of military power in the rebel States is a mere " whisper of fancy" or " vision of hope." On the contrary, it is capable of complete and speedy realization.

Overwhelm the rebel armies in the field, scatter them as organized bodies, dissipate their corps, divisions, brigades and regiments, and all other required results in this respect are easy of attainment. We are not to forget that in that case the Government of the United States would have a numerous, powerful, victorious army ready and desirous to *enforce the Constitution and the laws of their country, and to ensure domestic peace and tranquillity everywhere.* Moreover, none can be so willfully blind as not to see that in the *then existing* state of things the black male population of the rebel States would, under the control and guidance of our intelligent, patriotic and accomplished officers, of whom there is an abundance, furnish to the Government a physical force fully adequate to the sweeping away of every roving guerrilla and of effectually abolishing that inhuman and barbarous mode of warfare, and thus affording perfect protection, in every portion of the land, to the tribunals of justice in the exercise of their judicial duties and powers, and of securing everywhere the due and just execution of the " laws of the land." I advert to this effective and available force merely to show that as protection to the courts of justice would in the event supposed, be indispensable, so the Government would possess the undoubted physical power of furnishing that protection; while at the same time it is highly improbable that the necessity for using that power would ever arise. Why should it? At the period supposed, the rebel armies will have been driven from the field and their military power *as a people* will have ceased; they will be powerless as to sustaining even the semblance of military organization; without this, it will be palpable even to themselves, that further resistance to the Constitution and the laws would be wholly in vain; and taught as they already are by bitter experience, an experience the bitterness of which will daily from this hour to that become more and more intense, it is accordant with every dictate of human reason and every principle and motive of human action to believe, that *then* the scales will fall from the eyes of that people; that they will discern the error and delusion under which they have acted and that they will return to the blessed household of their and our fathers as cheerfully and fraternally as we shall welcome them back to it. I say "that people," in which term I do not include the *leading spirits of the rebellion*—the awful weight of moral guilt resting on them renders wholly and for ever impossible their admission to so pure and sacred a place as our "Temple of Liberty." What shall be their ultimate fate their own people may by that time be ready and willing to decide. It is thus seen, (1.) That the total annihilation of the military power of the rebellion is an indispensable pre-requisite to restoration. (2.) That that annihilation is practicable and, it may be added, certain.

The question will *then* directly arise, what is the condition of the rebel States, and with what rights, powers and privileges do they practically resume their place in the Union. I say *practically*, because *theoretically and legally* they have never been out of it. The answer to this question is easy to all who understand the principles of our complex political system, our "*imperia in imperio.*" That answer is, that they resume their place as members of the Union precisely as they were at the commencement of the rebellion, namely: with all their rights, powers and privileges as States subject to the great fundamental rule, *that the Constitution of the United States and all legislative and executive acts, pursuant to and in accordance with it, are the supreme law of the land,* and that to *that law* the Constitutions and laws of each State are subordinate.

4

They return to the Union, under and subject to the Constitution and to the laws and executive acts of the Government of the United States *accordant with the Constitution and then in force.*

This and this only is the true theory of restoration, the only mode by which the Constitution can be preserved for them and for us; in other words, the only salvation for the Government and the Union; the only safeguard against national disintegration; the only protection against anarchy and confusion and national ruin.   This being the rule and the principle, let us consider their operation practically. The Constitution speaks for itself; it stands unchanged and unchangeable (except in the mode itself prescribes): then the first inquiry will necessarily be, what laws and executive acts of the Government of the United States, *pursuant to and accordant with the Constitution,* are *then* in force? Such acts are, as already remarked, like the Constitution itself, the supreme law of the land—to them as to the Constitution, the Constitution and the laws of each State must yield.   In a practical point of view, the main acts of the kind alluded to, and which will then be of any material importance, are the Confiscation Act of Congress of July, 1862; the President's Proclamation pursuant thereto,* and the Emancipation

---

* A PROCLAMATION. By the President of the United States of America. In pursuance of the sixth section of the act of Congress entitled " An Act to suppress Insurrection, to punish Treason and Rebellion, to seize and confiscate the Property of Rebels, and for other purposes," approved July 17, 1862, and which act, and the joint resolution explanatory thereof, are herewith published, I, Abraham Lincoln, President of the United States, do hereby proclaim to and warn all persons within the contemplation of said sixth section to cease participating in, aiding, countenancing, or abetting in the existing rebellion, or any rebellion, against the Government of the United States, and to return to their proper allegiance to the United States, on pain of the forfeitures and seizures as within and by said sixth section provided.

In testimony whereof I have hereunto set my hand and caused the seal of the United States to be affixed.

    Done at the City of Washington, this 25th day of July, in the year of our Lord One [L. S.] Thousand Eight Hundred and Sixty-two, and of the Independence of the United States the Eighty-seventh.

By the President—WILLIAM H. SEWARD, Secretary of State.   ABRAHAM LINCOLN.

THE SIXTH SECTION.—Annexed is the sixth section of the Confiscation act referred to by the President in the above proclamation :

Sec. 6. *And be it further enacted,* That if any person within any State or Territory of the United States, other than those named as aforesaid, after the passage of this act, being engaged in armed rebellion against the Government of the United States, or aiding or abetting such rebellion, shall not, within sixty days after public warning and proclamation duly given and made by the President of the United States, cease to aid, countenance and abet such rebellion, and return to his allegiance to the United States, all the estates and property, moneys, stocks and credits of such person shall be liable to seizure as aforesaid, and it shall be the duty of the President to seize and use them as aforesaid, or the proceeds thereof. And all sales, transfers or conveyances of any such property after the expiration

Proclamations of the President of September, 1862,* and January,

of the said sixty days from the date of such warning and proclamation shall be null and void; and it shall be a sufficient bar to any suit brought by such person for the possession or the use of such property, or of any of it, to allege and prove that he is one of the persons described in this section.

* BY THE PRESIDENT OF THE UNITED STATES OF AMERICA.—*A Proclamation.* Washington, Sept. 22, 1862.—I, Abraham Lincoln, President of the United States of America, and Commander-in-Chief of the Army and Navy thereof, do hereby proclaim and declare that hereafter, as heretofore, the war will be prosecuted for the object of practically restoring the constitutional relation between the United States and the people thereof in which States that relation is, or may be, suspended or disturbed; that it is my purpose, upon the next meeting of Congress, to again recommend the adoption of a practical measure tendering pecuniary aid to the free acceptance or rejection of all the slave States, so-called, the people whereof may not then be in rebellion against the United States, and which States may then have voluntarily adopted or thereafter may voluntarily adopt the immediate or gradual abolishment of slavery within their respective limits; and that the efforts to colonize persons of African descent, with their consent, upon the continent or elsewhere, with the previously obtained consent of the Governments existing there, will be continued; that *on the first day of January, in the year of our Lord one thousand eight hundred and sixty-three, all persons held as slaves within any State, or any designated part of a State, the people whereof shall then be in rebellion against the United States, shall be then thenceforward and for ever free,* and the Executive Government of the United States, including the military and naval authority thereof, will recognize and maintain the freedom of such persons, and will do no act or acts to repress such persons, or any of them, in any efforts they may make for their actual freedom; that the Executive will, on the first day of January aforesaid, by proclamation, designate the States and parts of States, if any, in which the people thereof respectively shall then be in rebellion against the United States; and the fact that any State, or the people thereof, shall on that day be in good faith represented in the Congress of the United States by members chosen thereto at elections wherein a majority of the qualified voters of such State shall have participated, shall, in the absence of strong countervailing testimony, be deemed conclusive evidence that such State and the people thereof have not been in rebellion against the United States. That attention is hereby called to an act of Congress, entitled 'An Act to make an additional Article of War,' approved March 13, 1862, and which act is in the words and figures following: *Be it enacted by the Senate and House of Representatives of the United States of America in Congress assembled,* That hereafter the following shall be promulgated as an additional Article of War for the government of the Army of the United States, and shall be obeyed and observed as such: Article.—All officers or persons in the military or naval service of the United States are prohibited from employing any of the forces under their respective commands for the purpose of returning fugitives from service or labor who may have escaped from any persons to whom such service or labor is claimed to be due, and any officer who shall be found guilty by a court martial of violating this article shall be dismissed from the service. Section 2.—*And be it further enacted,* That this act shall take effect from and after its passage. Also to the ninth and tenth sections of an act entitled "An Act to suppress Insurrection, to punish Treason and Rebellion, to seize and Confiscate Property of Rebels, and for other purposes," approved July 17, 1862, and which sections are in the words and figures following: Section 9.—*And be it further enacted,* That all slaves of persons who shall hereafter be engaged in rebellion against the Government of the United States, or who shall in any way give aid or comfort thereto, escaping from such persons and taking refuge within the lines of the army, and all slaves captured by such persons, or deserted by them and coming under the control of the Government, and all slaves of such persons found on (or being within) any place occupied by rebel forces and afterwards occupied by the forces of the United States, shall be deemed captures of war, and shall be for ever free of their servitude, and not again held as slaves. Section 10.—*And be it further enacted,* That no slave escaping into any State, Territory, or the District of Columbia, from any of the States, shall be delivered up,

1863.* There are some other kindred acts and resolutions of Congress, but the above are fully sufficient for all purposes of illustration. By these it will be seen that assuming their *constitutional validity* the results are as follows: The real and personal property of all persons engaged in armed rebellion against the Government, or aiding or abetting the rebellion after the 25th of September, 1862, is liable to seizure and confiscation; and all sales and transfers made by such persons after that day are void.

All persons held as slaves on the 1st day of January, 1863, in the States of Arkansas, Texas, Mississippi, Alabama, Florida, Georgia, North Carolina, South Carolina, Virginia, (except fifty-five counties designated in the Proclamation of January 1, 1863,) and Louisiana, (except thirteen parishes designated in the same Proclamation,) are for ever free.

or in any way impeded or hindered of his liberty, except for some crime or offense against the laws, unless the person claiming said fugitive shall first make oath that the person to whom the labor or service of such fugitive is alleged to be due is his lawful owner, and has not been in arms against the United States in the present rebellion, nor in any way giving aid and comfort thereto; and no person engaged in the military or naval service of the United States shall, under any pretense whatever, assume to decide on the validity of the claim of any person to the service or labor of any other person, or surrender up any such person to the claimant, on pain of being dismissed from the service. And I do hereby enjoin upon and order all persons engaged in the military and naval service of the United States to observe, obey and enforce within their respective spheres of service the act and sections above recited. And the Executive will in due time recommend that all citizens of the United States who shall have remained loyal thereto throughout the rebellion shall (upon the restoration of the constitutional relation between the United States and their respective States and people, if the relation shall have been suspended or disturbed,) be compensated for all losses by acts of the United States, including the loss of slaves. In witness whereof I have hereunto set my hand and caused the seal of the United States to be affixed.

                                                                    ABRAHAM LINCOLN.

* WASHINGTON, Jan. 1, 1863. By the President of the United States of America.—*A Proclamation.*—Whereas, on the Twenty-second day of September, in the year of Our Lord One Thousand Eight Hundred and Sixty-two, a Proclamation was issued by the President of the United States containing among other things the following to wit:

"That on the first day of January, in the year of Our Lord One Thousand Eight Hundred and Sixty-three, all persons held as slaves within any State, or designated part of a State, the people whereof shall then be in rebellion against the United States, shall be then thenceforth and FOR EVER FREE, and the Executive Government of the United States, including the military and naval authorities thereof, will recognize and maintain the freedom of such persons, and will do no act or acts to repress such persons, or any of them, in any effort they may make for their actual freedom. That the Executive will, on the first day of January aforesaid, by proclamation, designate the States and parts of States, if any, in which the people therein respectively shall then be in rebellion against the United States, and the fact that any State, or the people thereof, shall on that day be in good faith represented in the Congress of the United States by members chosen thereto at elections wherein a majority of the qualified voters of such States shall have participated, shall, in the absence of strong countervailing testimony, be deemed conclusive evidence that such State and the people thereof are not then in rebellion against the United States." Now therefore, I,

This is not the time nor the place for the discussion of the question of the constitutional validity of those acts.

On a former occasion, I endeavored to show that the Proclamation of September, 1862, was a constitutional exercise of Presidential power, and that it would legally and constitutionally produce its intended effects. Others take the opposite view, and as to the constitutional validity of the legislative act just referred to able arguments have been made on both sides. But those arguments on either side are practically unimportant, for they *decide* nothing.

But, fortunately for our country, there is a tribunal possessing full power to adjudicate these all-important questions authoritatively and conclusively. That tribunal is the Supreme Court of the United States; and to its judgments we must all, North and South, East and West, bow submissively. It will be the province of that august tribunal to pronounce judgment on these momentous questions—and to that judgment the fanatical Abolitionist * of the

Abraham Lincoln, President of the United States, by virtue of the power in me vested as Commander-in-Chief of the Army and Navy of the United States in time of actual armed rebellion against the authority and Government of the United States, and as a fit and necessary war measure for suppressing said rebellion, do, on this first day of January in the year of Our Lord One Thousand Eight Hundred and Sixty-three, and in accordance with my purpose so to do, publicly proclaim for the full period of one hundred days from the day of the first above-mentioned order, and designate, as the States and parts of States wherein the people thereof respectively are this day in rebellion against the United States, the following, to wit: Arkansas, Texas, Louisiana—except the Parishes of St. Bernard, Plaquemine, Jefferson, St. John, St. Charles, St. James, Ascension, Assumption, Terre Bonne, Lafourche, St. Mary, St. Martin and Orleans, including the city of New-Orleans—Mississippi, Alabama, Florida, Georgia, South Carolina, and Virginia—except the forty-eight counties designated as West Virginia, and also the counties of Berkley, Accomac, Northampton, Elizabeth City, York, Princess Anne, and Norfolk, including the cities of Norfolk and Portsmouth, and which excepted parts are, for the present, left precisely as if this proclamation was not issued. And by virtue of the power and for the purpose aforesaid, I do order and declare that all persons held as slaves within said designated States and parts of States are, and henceforward shall be free! and that the Executive Government of the United States, including the military and naval authorities thereof will recognize and maintain the freedom of said persons. And I hereby enjoin upon the people so declared to be free, to abstain from all violence, unless in necessary self-defense, and I recommend to them that in all cases, when allowed, they labor faithfully for reasonable wages. And I faithfully declare and make known that such persons of suitable condition will be received into the armed service of the United States for garrisoning forts, positions, stations and other places, and to man vessels of all sorts in said service. And upon this, sincerely believed to be an act of justice, warranted by the Constitution, upon military necessity, I invoke the considerate judgment of mankind and the gracious favor of Almighty God. In witness whereof I have hereunto set my hand and caused the seal of the United States to be affixed. Done at the City of Washington, this first day of January, in the year of Our Lord One Thousand [L. S.] Eight Hundred and Sixty-three, and of the Independence of the United States of America the Eighty-seventh. ABRAHAM LINCOLN.

* By this term I mean those men, who believe and have declared that the " Constitution is a league with hell and a covenant with the devil," and who would sacrifice the Union,

North and the fanatical pro-slavery man of the South will be compelled to yield implicit, if not cheerful, obedience.   I have already
shown that, contemporaneously with the total annihilation of the
military power of the States in rebellion, will arise the power peace-
fully to bring into full effect the Constitution and laws of the Union
through her judicial tribunals.   On the arrival of that period, those
various questions will be presented and, in due and regular course
and form of law, be conducted to a final decision.   If we suppose
that decision to affirm the constitutional validity of those several
executive and legislative acts, then indeed *existing* slavery ceases in
the rebel States* and sundry losses in other respects fall on individuals there.   But they and the whole world will know and remember that these consequences, calamitous as the sufferers may
deem them to be, are the legitimate effects of their attempt to overthrow their Government ; they will then learn, as millions before
them have learned, that the " way of the transgressor is hard."

rather than not carry into full execution their plan of absolute and universal negro emancipation.   This class is not numerous—indeed, as already stated in the text, it was originally
and still is ludicrously small.   The only *practical* effect produced by them has been, as I
have mentioned, the furnishing the rebel conspirators, by means of extracts from " Abolition" speeches and publications the means of fiery appeals to the ignorance, prejudice and
credulity of their people and thus to prepare them for plunging into the rebellion.   It may
be said that this " Abolition" fanaticism is the fanaticism of humanity and philanthropy,
and that the rebel fanaticism is the fanaticism of barbarism and cruelty ; if this be granted,
the fact still remains that each fanaticism is equally inimical to the country, and would equally
rejoice at the downfall of the Constitution, *if its ends could not otherwise be attained.*

* Much has been said and written during the last half century as to the barbarizing effects
of slavery, as it exists and is practised in the rebel States, on the white race born and nur-
tured under its influence.   Tens of thousands among us have listened with incredulity to
those statements, but the revelations of the war of the rebellion have convinced the most
sceptical of their truth.   Innumerable have been the well-authenticated instances, since the
commencement of the rebellion, of every refinement of cruelty inflicted on Union citizens
and soldiers by armed and unarmed rebels.   It is due to the truth of history to record a few
out of the multitudes of these outrages on humanity.   Prominent on the list stands the
" Fort Pillow massacre."   As to this, we have the most reliable evidence in the report of the
Committee of Congress appointed to investigate the matter (Senator Wade and Representa-
tive Gooch).   The report was submitted to Congress on the 5th of May, 1864, and, among
other things, states : " It appears from the testimony that the atrocities committed at Fort
Pillow were not the result of passions excited by the heat of conflict, but were the results
of a policy deliberately decided on and unhesitatingly announced.   Here the brutality and
cruelty of the rebels were most painfully exhibited.   The garrison consisted of 19 officers
and 538 men, of whom 262 were colored troops, comprising one battalion of the 6th United
States heavy artillery (formerly called the 1st Alabama artillery), of colored troops, under
command of Major L. F. Booth ; one section of the 2d United States light artillery, colored,
and one battalion of the 13th Tennessee cavalry, white, commanded by Major W. F. Bradford.   Major Booth was the ranking officer, and was in command of the post.   On Tuesday,
the 12th of April (the anniversary of the attack on Fort Sumter, in April, 1861), the pickets
of the garrison were driven in just about sunrise, that being the first intimation our forces
there had of any intention on the part of the enemy to attack that place.   Fighting soon be-

I have said "existing slavery," for no power is found in the Constitution to prevent any State from hereafter arranging its domestic institutions as it may see fit; and consequently there is no power to inhibit future slavery in the rebel or in any States. But if all the slaves now in those States are legally free by reason of the legislative and executive acts above mentioned, each of those States is, after the decision of the Supreme Court to that effect, without a slave within its

came general, and about 9 o'clock Major Booth was killed. Major Bradford succeeded to the command, and withdrew all the forces within the fort. They had previously occupied some intrenchments at some distance from the fort, and further from the river. This fort was situated on a high bluff, which descended precipitately to the river's edge, the side of the bluff on the river's side being covered with trees, bushes, and fallen timber. Extending back from the river, on either side of the fort, was a ravine or hollow—the one below the fort containing several private stores and some dwellings, constituting what was called the town. At the mouth of that ravine, and on the river bank, were some Government buildings, containing commissary and quartermaster's stores. The ravine above the fort was known as Cold Creek ravine, the sides being covered with trees and bushes. To the right, or below and a little to the front of the fort, was a level piece of ground, not quite so elevated as the fort itself, on which had been erected some log huts or shanties, which were occupied by the white troops, and also used for hospital and other purposes. Within the fort, tents had been erected, with board floors, for the use of the colored troops. There were six pieces of artillery in the fort, consisting of two 6-pounder howitzers, and two 10-pounder Parrots. The rebels continued their attack, but up to two or three o'clock in the afternoon, they had not gained any decisive success. Our troops, both white and black, fought most bravely, and were in good spirits. The gunboat No. 7 (New Era), Captain Marshall, took part in the conflict, shelling the enemy as opportunity offered. Signals had been agreed upon by which the officers in the fort could indicate where the guns of the boat could be most effective. There being but one gunboat there, no permanent impression appears to have been produced upon the enemy; for, as they were shelled out of one ravine, they would make their appearance in the other. They would thus appear and retire as the gunboat moved from one point to the other. About one o'clock the fire on both sides slackened somewhat, and the gunboat moved out in the river, to cool and clean its guns, having fired 282 rounds of shell, shrapnel and canister, which nearly exhausted its supply of ammunition. The rebels having thus far failed in their attack, now resorted to their customary use of flags of truce. The first flag of truce conveyed a demand from Forrest for the unconditional surrender of the fort. To this Major Bradford replied, asking to be allowed one hour to consult with his officers and the officers of the gunboat. In a short time a second flag of truce appeared, with a communication from Forrest, that he would allow Major Bradford twenty minutes in which to move his troops out of the fort, and if it was not done within that time an assault would be ordered. To this Major Bradford returned the reply that he would not surrender. During the time these flags of truce were flying, the rebels were moving down the ravine and taking positions from which the more readily to charge upon the fort. Parties of them were also engaged in plundering the Government buildings of commissary and quartermaster's stores, in full view of the gunboat. Captain Marshall states that he refrained from firing upon the rebels, although they were thus violating the flag of truce, for fear that, should they finally succeed in capturing the fort, they would justify any atrocities they might commit by saying that they were in retaliation for his firing while the flag of truce was flying. He says, however, that when he saw the rebels coming down the ravine above the fort, and taking positions there, he got under way and stood for the fort, determined to use what little ammunition he had left in shelling them out of the ravine; but he did not get up within effective range before the final assault was made. Immediately after the second flag of truce retired, the rebels made a rush from the positions they had so treacherously gained and obtained possession of the fort, raising the

borders. In that state of things the intensest enemy of slavery would feel no anxiety for the future, for he would know that by no act of legislation of any State could those, who had become free, be again reduced to slavery; and he would also know, that in order to the re-introduction of slavery in any State, legislative acts for that purpose must be enacted. The enactment of such acts would be most improbable in view of the present state of opinion throughout the

cry of ' No quarter !' But little opportunity was allowed for our resistance. Our troops, black and white, threw down their arms, and sought to escape by running down the steep bluff near the fort, and secreting themselves behind trees and logs, in the bushes, and under the brush—some even jumping into the river, leaving only their heads above the water, as they crouched down under the bank. Then followed a scene of cruelty and murder without a parallel in civilized warfare, which needed but the tomahawk and scalping-knife to exceed the worst atrocities ever committed by savages. The rebels commenced an indiscriminate slaughter, sparing neither age nor sex, white or black, soldier or civilian. The officers and men seemed to vie with each other in the devilish work; men, women, and even children, wherever found, were deliberately shot down, beaten, and hacked with sabres; some of the children not more than ten years old were forced to stand up and face their murderers while being shot; the sick and the wounded were butchered without mercy, the rebels even entering the hospital building and dragging them out to be shot, or killing them as they lay there unable to offer the least resistance. All over the hillside the work of murder was going on; numbers of our men were collected together in lines or groups and deliberately shot; some were shot while in the river, while others on the bank were shot and their bodies kicked into the water, many of them still living but unable to make any exertion to save themselves from drowning. Some of the rebels stood on the top of the hill or a short distance down its side, and called to our soldiers to come up to them, and as they approached, shot them down in cold blood; if their guns or pistols missed fire, forcing them to stand there until they were again prepared to fire. All around were heard cries of ' No quarter !' ' No quarter !' ' Kill the damned niggers; shoot them down !' All who asked for mercy were answered by the most cruel taunts and sneers. Some were spared for a time only to be murdered under circumstances of greater cruelty. No cruelty which the most fiendish malignity could devise was omitted by these murderers. One white soldier who was wounded in one leg so as to be unable to walk, was made to stand up while his tormentors shot him; others who were wounded and unable to stand were held up and again shot. One negro who had been ordered by a rebel officer to hold his horse, was killed by him when he remounted; another, a mere child, whom an officer had taken up behind him on his horse, was seen by Chalmers, who at once ordered the officer to put him down and shoot him, which was done. The huts and tents in which many of the wounded had taken shelter were set on fire, both that night and the next morning, while the wounded were still in them—those only escaping who were able to get themselves out, or who could prevail on others less injured than themselves to help them out; and even some of those thus seeking to escape the flames were met by those ruffians and brutally shot down, or had their brains beaten out. One man was deliberately fastened down to the floor of a tent, face upwards, by means of nails driven through his clothing and into the boards under him, so that he could not possibly escape, and then the tent set on fire; another was nailed to a building outside of the fort, and then the building set on fire and burned. The charred remains of five or six bodies were afterwards found, all but one so much disfigured and consumed by the flames that they could not be identified, and the identification of that one is not absolutely certain, although there can hardly be a doubt that it was the body of Lieutenant Akerstrom, Quartermaster of the 13th Tennessee cavalry, and a native Tennessean; several witnesses who saw the remains, and who were personally acquainted with him while living, have testified that it is their firm belief that it was his body that was thus treated. These deeds of murder and cruelty ceased when night came

world; in view of the effect of the war on the slaves themselves as before mentioned; in view of the fact that the slave trade is piracy; and of the further fact, that at the period in question the only slaves in our country would be the comparatively few remaining in the border slave States, and in the excepted counties and parishes above mentioned. Under such circumstances, the passage of an act re-establishing slavery would be a purely idle ceremony. Thus it is seen that such a decision on this point would in no manner infringe on State rights and privileges present or prospective. On the other hand, let us suppose that the decision of the Supreme judicial tribunal of the Union is adverse to the validity of the acts in

on, only to be renewed the next morning, when the demons carefully sought among the dead lying about in all directions for any of the wounded yet alive, and those they found were deliberately shot. Scores of the dead and wounded were found there the day after the massacre by the men from some of our gunboats who were permitted to go on shore and collect the wounded and bury the dead. The rebels themselves had made a pretense of burying a great many of their victims, but they had merely thrown them, without the least regard to care or decency, into the trenches and ditches about the fort, or the little hollows and ravines on the hillside, covering them but partially with earth. Portions of heads and faces, hands and feet, were found protruding through the earth in every direction. The testimony also establishes the fact that the rebels buried some of the living with the dead, a few of whom succeeded afterwards in digging themselves out, or were dug out by others, one of whom your committee found in Mound City hospital, and there examined. And even when your committee visited the spot, two weeks afterwards, although parties of men had been sent on shore from time to time to bury the bodies unburied and re-bury the others, and were even then engaged in the same work, we found the evidences of this murder and cruelty still more painfully apparent; we saw bodies still unburied (at some distance from the fort) of some sick men who had been met fleeing from the hospital and beaten down and brutally murdered, and their bodies left where they had fallen. We could still see the faces, hands, and feet of men, white and black, protruding out of the ground, whose graves had not been reached by those engaged in re-interring the victims of the massacre; and although a great deal of rain had fallen within the preceding two weeks, the ground, more especially on the side and at the foot of the bluff where the most of the murders had been committed, was still discolored by the blood of our brave but unfortunate men, and the logs and trees showed but too plainly the evidences of the atrocities perpetrated there. Many other instances of equally atrocious cruelty might be enumerated, but your committee feel compelled to refrain from giving here more of the heart-sickening details, and refer to the statements contained in the voluminous testimony herewith submitted. These statements were obtained by them from eye-witnesses and sufferers; many of them, as they were examined by your committee, were lying upon beds of suffering, some so feeble that their lips could with difficulty frame the words by which they endeavored to convey some idea of the cruelties which had been inflicted on them, and which they had seen inflicted on others. How many of our troops thus fell victims to the malignity and barbarity of Forrest and his followers cannot yet be definitely ascertained. Two officers belonging to the garrison were absent at the time of the capture and massacre. Of the remaining officers but two are known to be living, and they are wounded and now in the hospital at Mound City. One of them, Captain Potter, may even now be dead, as the surgeons, when your committee were there, expressed no hope of his recovery. Of the men, from 300 to 400 are known to have been killed at Fort Pillow, of whom, at least, 300 were murdered in cold blood after the post was in possession of the rebels, and our men had thrown down their arms and ceased to offer resistance. Of the survivors, except the

question and consequently that they produce none of their intended
effects. In that event, the zealous anti-slavery man must content
himself with the hope that, though the institution he so cordially
hates has not been destroyed by law, but still in a legal sense exists, yet that the war of the rebellion has in reality given it its
death-blow, and that after a few years of lingering it will disappear
for ever. But whether the pro-slavery man on the one side, or the
anti-slavery man on the other, is satisfied with the irreversible judgment of that tribunal is of no moment; the patriot, in whatever
section of the land he may be found, rejoices that the *Constitution*
has been preserved, and that its foundations, instead of having been
shaken by rebels on the one side or "Abolitionists" on the other,
are firmer and stronger than ever.

wounded in the hospital at Mound City, and the few who succeeded in making their escape
unhurt, nothing definite is known ; and it is to be feared that many have been murdered
after being taken away from the fort. In reference to the fate of Major Bradford, who was
in command of the fort when it was captured, and who had up to that time received no
injury, there seems to be no doubt. The general understanding everywhere seemed to be
that he had been brutally murdered the day after he was taken prisoner. There is some
discrepancy in the testimony, but your committee do not see how the one who professed to
have been an eye-witness of his death could have been mistaken. There may be some
uncertainty in regard to his fate. When your committee arrived at Memphis, Tennessee,
they found and examined a man (Mr. McLagan,) who had been conscripted by some of
Forrest's forces, but who, with other conscripts, had succeeded in making his escape. He
testifies that while two companies of rebel troops, with Major Bradford and many other
prisoners, were on their march from Brownsville to Jackson, Tennessee, Major Bradford
was taken by five rebels—one an officer—led about fifty yards from the line of march, and
deliberately murdered in view of all there assembled. He fell—killed instantly by three
musket balls, even while asking that his life might be spared, as he had fought them man-
fully, and was deserving of a better fate. The motive for the murder of Major Bradford
seems to have been the simple fact that, although a native of the South, he remained loyal
to his Government. The testimony herewith submitted contains many statements made
by the rebels, that they did not intend to treat ' home-made Yankees,' as they termed loyal
Southerners, any better than negro troops." Such horrors scarcely find a parallel in the
dreadful atrocities of the Sepoys of India in their late rebellion against the British Government.

The treatment of Union prisoners in the dungeons of Richmond is universally known to
have been and still to be cruel and inhuman to a degree unparalleled. Instances almost
innumerable could be stated. I will confine myself to an official letter from Gov. Brough,
of Ohio:

The State of Ohio, Executive Department, *Columbus, May 3, 1864.*—Sir— I have your
favor of the 19th inst. All prisoners of war, civil and military, are under the sole charge
of Col. Wm. Hoffman, Commissary General of prisoners, Washington City. I cannot interfere with them if I would, and I cannot give an order to see or communicate with them,
without his permission. I am glad it is so. Some four weeks ago I saw at Baltimore the
arrival of a vessel loaded with our prisoners from Belle Isle, who, in the very refinement of
barbarism, had been reduced by starvation to mere skeletons, for no other purpose than to
incapacitate them for service in the Union armies. Over one-third of these men were too
far gone to be resuscitated, and died within forty-eight hours after their arrival. While I
would not retaliate on rebel prisoners by practising like means, I confess, General, I have

Thus, while no plan of restoration, which implies a territorial condition on the part of the rebel States or which requires or justifies any interference in the local affairs or local governments of those States as States, is demanded by necessity, so no such plan can receive the sanction of any, who adhere to the fundamental, and the only true and safe principle, namely, that at all hazards and in all events, the Constitution must be preserved *inviolate*. On the ground now stated, the "straitest sect" of strict construction-

very little sympathy with or desire to parole or release from confinement men who have been upholding a rebellion that has deluged the land with sorrow and blood, and whose leaders have resorted to cruelty and barbarism in the treatment of prisoners more infernal than ever practised by savages. The higher the rank and social position of men, the less are they entitled to sympathy. They sinned against light and knowledge. Therefore, I am glad their fate is not in my keeping, lest under such provocation I should not be over merciful.   JOHN BROUGH."

I select from the hundreds of similar published statements the following, because I know the writer and can vouch for his truth and integrity : " I was living in the north part of Texas when the rebellion broke out, and, with my loyal friends, did all in my power to oppose it. For this we were often threatened to be hung. In the Summer of 1860 many towns were destroyed by fire in Texas, supposed to be the work of Abolition incendiaries. But after the war broke out it was ascertained for a fact that the towns burned were set on fire by some of the ringleaders of the rebel party for the purpose of exciting the people against the North and uniting them in the rebellion. In 1862 Arkansas and Texas were declared under martial law ; and woe to the loyal people, for now their troubles had just begun ! Any man accused of disloyalty to the confederacy would be arrested and tried before the Provost Marshal and hung, in many cases, in less than six hours from the time of their arrest ! In the month of October, 1862, over one hundred of my loyal friends suffered in this way. *Twenty-two were hung at the same time, one morning before breakfast, without the least shadow of a trial*, by order of James Young, a captain in the rebel army. Several of the loyal men attempted to escape to the Federal lines. Some succeeded, but many were captured and shot down or hung like dogs. I was followed for three hundred and fifty miles, and after many hair-breadth escapes, succeeded in passing nearly all the rebel pickets in the north part of Arkansas, when I was arrested by the rebel soldiers on suspicion of attempting to escape to the 'enemy's country,' (as they termed it,) and sent to Little Rock under a strong guard, and confined in an iron cage twelve feet square, inside of a filthy and sickly prison ; but I was not alone. Several other Union men were there before me, part of whom were taken out and executed. Others died of diseases contracted in prison ; and others were taken out and forced into the rebel army ; and still others were suffered to remain there without any trial or investigation, kept in bitter suspense, not knowing what hour a guard might call for some of us to accompany them to the suburbs of the city where many a loyal man has been sent to his 'long home.' Wives of loyal men who had been arrested on suspicion and torn from their families, would come to Little Rock and visit the prison in search of their husbands, and in many cases find that they had been either executed or died in prison ! Such agony and groans as I have witnessed from these heart-broken widows are enough to freeze the blood in one's veins ! A true history of the rebellion in the South is one of blood, barbarism and savage ferocity, which perhaps can never be written.   FRED. W. SUMNER."

In all the European wars of the last one hundred years, in our wars of the Revolution and of 1812, in our war with Mexico, no such acts of cruelty and barbarity occurred. I do not make the foregoing extracts to excite bitterness of feeling or to arouse indignation--but merely to suggest that the fall of the institution of slavery, if such is to be its fate, will not

ists of the Constitution and of liberal constructionists of State rights can stand in common with him who has the most latitudinarian views of the Constitution and the most narrow idea of State power and sovereignty; for they will all agree as on axiomatic truths, that the Constitution must in no manner be violated; that the Constitution and all legislative and executive acts in harmony with it are the supreme law of the land; that the Supreme Court of the United States is invested with the power to pass authoritatively and conclusively on the questions now under consideration.

It cannot, I think, be doubted that the great body of the people of the States not in rebellion are earnestly and intelligently attached to our institutions, and would on no condition assent to their downfall.* Those of native descent revere and honor the memory of their fathers; they cling with heartfelt affection to their traditions, and they will never knowingly connive at or participate in the destruction of the great and sacred work commenced by them by the Revolution and consummated by the Constitution. They in their heart of hearts love and cherish that work. Citizens of foreign birth have, if possible, more imperative and resistless reasons for cherishing those institutions and preserving them for ever inviolate; for in them they have found a safe and happy refuge from the tyranny of other lands, from the depressing influences of aristocratic systems, the social depression of " class" and " caste," from grinding poverty and practical slavery. They will never *understandingly* assent to their annihilation.

cause tears of regret to flow any where, if indeed this conduct of the people and the soldiers of the rebel States can be accounted for on no principle or theory except the necessary influence of their social system on the hearts and dispositions of their population. Probably an additional explanation of the enigma may be found, as some one has suggested, in the idea that it is the legitimate and necessary fruit of the radical and desperate wickedness of the cause in which they are engaged.

* I have said that it was the firm resolve of the great bulk of our people to crush the rebellion. The considerations already stated would seem conclusive on this subject, but it would be gross injustice to my countrymen, to omit to mention the constant and the costly offerings they have *individually* made and are still making in this cause. The records of all history furnish no more illustrious examples of patriotic devotion and of real philanthropy, of unselfish benevolence and genuine humanity. To say nothing of the vast expenditures of the Government as such, let us look at the offerings of our citizens individually and in States, counties, towns, cities and neighborhoods.

It is stated on competent authority, (" *Philanthropic Results of the War in America*,' Sheldon & Co., New York,) that up to February, 1864, these contributions were as follows:

(1.) Expended by the *States* for the equipment and maintenance of troops, not reimbursed or promised to be reimbursed by the General Government, $10,937,323.

(2.) Bounties, extra pay, and allowances to families of Volunteers (by State,) $47,585,-500.

How is it, then, that so many among us, both native and naturalized, are found in apparent sympathy with the rebellion; or, if not in sympathy with it, indifferent apparently to its result? The vast majority of the persons now alluded to would be shocked to believe that they were not the country's real friends and supporters; to such the terms "disloyal," "traitor," do not apply and their indiscriminate use is equally unjustified by fact and repugnant to policy and good sense. Some few among us are undoubtedly disloyal and desire the success of the rebellion, while with mean hypocrisy and cowardice they profess patriotism; but such anomalies are, gratefully be it said, not numerous. I cannot waste time on them. Now and then one is found (as I have incidentally mentioned,) who is really honest, because *he* candidly admits that he considers man incapable of self-government and therefore prefers a monarchy or oligarchy to a Republic. The number of those is but as a drop in our great ocean. Why, then, I ask again, is it that there are many who, though they do not in reality sympathize with the rebellion, yet in their expressions of opinion and in their actions, give hope and encouragement to the rebels and impede in a greater or less degree the efforts for their overthrow? This question admits, I think, of but one answer; from the very nature of the case there can be but one explanation, and that is, that those persons do not understand, or fail to remember, that the re-

(3.) By cities, towns, corporations and individuals for raising and recruiting regiments, aside from bounties and relief to families, $34,230,000.

(4.) By counties, towns, cities, corporations and individuals, for bounties and aid to families of Volunteers, $79,595,743.

(5.) By State, contribution for sick and wounded soldiers, in different for as, $346,041.

(6.) By State, contributions for National defense, not included under any of the foregoing heads, $13,010,000.

(7.) By individuals, contributions for the general purposes of National defense, *not enumerated above*, $1,005,000.

(8.) By associations and individuals, contributions for the care and support of soldiers, whether in camp or sick and wounded and for their families, $24,041,535.

(9.) By associations and individuals, contributions for freedmen and white Union refugees, $532,144.

The details are all given in the work referred to.

The contribution noticed above include in part those made up to the 1st of February last, through those magnificent monuments of a "Christian" age, the United States Sanitary Commission and the United States Christian Commission. The receipts of the former up to the 1st of July, 1864, in money and property were about $15,000,000, and of the latter $2,500,000. Whatever of military renown or prestige the American people may have acquired by this war, the philanthropist will consider all that eclipsed by these extraordinary manifestations of charity and benevolence.

In view of all the facts stated in this note, may it not well be said that a people, capable of such works, are incapable of *surrendering to treason and rebellion ! !*

bellion was wholly and absolutely causeless, as the facts incontro-
vertibly show; they do not know or they fail to appreciate its true
and real causes and origin, the *secret motives* which influenced its
originators and their intentions and designs, as to which there is no
room for doubt, if we look at the irrefragable testimony already ad-
duced; and above all, they are wholly blind to the inevitably fatal
results of the rebellion (if successful,) to our national existence and
to the cause of "civil liberty" and "free institutions" now and for
ever. Those results I have candidly and truly stated. It is necessarily impossible for any man (whatever may be his intellectual
ability) to think, or reason, or write *correctly* on this momentous
subject unless he understands, realizes and appreciates the facts
just adverted to. *With that pre-requisite,* however severely he may
condemn various acts of the *Administration,* civil and military,
and however strongly he may express that condemnation, he will
not endanger the great cause by giving "aid and comfort" to the
rebellion. Without it, he becomes, imperceptibly to himself practically an enemy of the Union and a friend of the rebellion.*

VII.

In view of existing facts already stated, the inevitable conclusion is, that the rebellion *will be crushed* and that our country will
be saved. When that blessed event shall happen, when it is pro-
claimed that the war of the rebellion is ended and that our country throughout all its borders is again under the beneficent domin-
ion of the Constitution and the laws, what will then be the condition
of the United States and what the future before them?

We shall have triumphantly passed through a war of more gigan-
tic proportions than any that has preceded it, considering the multitudes of men on either side that have been engaged and have

---

* This truth is mournfully illustrated in a late publication entitled "The Future." Its
author is an intelligent and respectable gentleman and believes himself patriotic. His
case is the more singular from the fact that the rebellion has taken the life of his near and
cherished relative, a youthful hero who fell nobly fighting for the Republic in the second
year of the rebellion. Yet the whole *animus* of this publication is inimical to his country
and sympathetic with her enemies and is well calculated to give them "comfort" and encouragement. *If they succeed they will not forget the favor* received at his hands. Let the
mantle of charity be cast over him; and let us hope, when the not distant hour arrives which
shall witness our triumph over treason and rebellion, that his countrymen amid their
rejoicings will forgive the grievous wrongs he and others like him have done, "for they
know not what they do."

fallen in it, the number of truly *great* battles that have been fought, the thousands of millions of treasure that have been required to maintain and conduct it. We shall have brought this mighty struggle to a successful and a glorious end! We shall have exhibited to the world innumerable instances of individual patriotic sacrifice and of sublime heroism. We shall have furnished to history its most beautiful page in the relation she will give of the philanthropy and benevolence of our citizens.* We shall have proved to all nations that we are a people of unsurpassed, I do not say unequaled, moral and physical courage, and that we are the worthy inheritors of the priceless institutions transmitted to us by our fathers; and above all, we shall have demonstrated the great truth —*that man is capable of self-government.*

Some apprehend that the close of the war of the rebellion will find us encumbered with a debt, under which we must struggle and fall. But a few plain facts will show how wholly unfounded is this apprehension. I advance no fanciful nor exaggerated proposition when I say, that no country in Christendom possesses the *material means* that by the favor of God belong to us, and no country is more able to bear the burden that is thus devolved upon us. And yet one country certainly (Great Britain, if not others,) has for a long time readily sustained and now sustains an equal burden. We can and we shall sustain it. Few even among us, and fewer abroad, are aware of the extent of our resources. Let us consider these for a moment.

(1.) Our population in 1860 was 31,445,080. The increase in every decade since 1790, has been nearly thirty-five per cent. The Superintendent of the Census (Mr. Kennedy), in his compend, published in 1862, estimates the population in 1870 at 42,318,432; and in 1880, at 56,450,241; and if this rate of increase continues, we shall number in sixty years from this day, over 200,000,000.

(2.) We have derived, and shall continue to derive from *immigration* an immense annual addition to our physical power and financial resources. Mr. Kennedy, in his preliminary report to the census of 1860, states the whole number of emigrants to this country from 1820 to 1860, at five and one half millions. Notwithstanding the war of the rebellion, no stop has been put to immigration; on the contrary, the arrivals during the past year show a large increase;

---

* A preceding note shows the munificence of the patriotic and benevolent offerings which have been made. The Sanitary and the Christian Commission, are the " glory " of the age, the " shining lights " of the Nineteenth Century.

and the American Consul at Liverpool, in a letter of the 22d of April last, to our Secretary of State, says, that the immigration at this time from that port to the United States is unprecedented ; that there are not half ships enough to carry the emigrants waiting for a passage, and that he was informed by one firm in that city, that they alone could send to us within two months, 50,000 persons if they had ships to convey them. That this immigration will be enormously increased, on the suppression of the rebellion, cannot be doubted. Not to speak of the numerical addition thus made to our population, the addition by this means to the wealth and financial ability of the nation is correspondently great. The reports of the Emigrant Commissioners of the State of New York show that the average amount of money brought by immigrants, in addition to their personal effects, contributed sensibly to the extraordinary rapid increase of our personal property, as exhibited by successive censuses. Besides, every man contributes by his productive labor to our national wealth, and he contributes to the national treasury in the way of taxation and per centage on the food he eats, the clothes he wears, and the luxuries, if any, he enjoys. It is a low estimate to assume that each man adds $100 per year to the national wealth, and $10 a year to the national treasury. We have, then, in immigration a perennial, essential increase of ability to bear our pecuniary burdens.

(3.) The official valuation of the property of our country in 1860 was $16,159,616,068 ; or deducting the value of slaves, $14,223,618,068, being an increase over the valuation of 1850 of more than $8,000,000,000 (eight billions). Thus, the increase of *property* in this decade was 130 per cent., while that of population but little exceeds 35 per cent. The valuation at this time would greatly exceed that of four years ago.

(4.) The United States embrace a territorial area of 2,936,166 square miles, or 1,879,146,240 acres,[of which in May, 1863, there remained undisposed of and belonging to the Government of the United States, 964,901,625 acres,]extending from the 24th to the 49th degrees of north latitude, and from the 67th to the 125th of west longitude and lying between the two great oceans of the world, it embraces every variety of climate and of soil and is capable of every variety of production.* Of the immense quantity of land of

---

* " The area of all the valleys which are drained by the rivers of Europe which empty into the Atlantic, all the valleys which are drained by the rivers of Asia which empty into

which the Government still remains the owner, the very large proportion is capable of cultivation.

(5.) Our agricultural productions are on a corresponding scale. In the eight interior States extending from the Western bounds of Pennsylvania and New York to the Missouri River, and from the Ohio River north to the British dominions, the cereal productions in 1860 were 588,160,323 bushels, exceeding the whole annual product of England, and about equal to that of France. The cattle numbered 7,204,810; the swine, 11,039,352; these, it will be remembered, are the products of only eight of our States. The number of barrels of wheat and flour carried on the Erie Canal to the Hudson River in 1862 was 7,516,397.

(6.) Our mineral productions are inestimable in value and exhaustless in quantity. Our coal is stated by Sir William Armstrong, to be thirty-two times as great in quantity as that of the United Kingdom; and our iron bears a similar proportion. The Commissioner of the General Land Office in his official report of December 29, 1862, says:

" The great auriferous region of the United States, in the western portion of the continent stretches from the 49th degree of north latitude and Puget Sound, to the 30° 30'' parallel, and from the 102d degree of longitude west of Greenwich to the Pacific ocean, embracing portions of Dakota, Nebraska, Colorado, all of New Mexico, with Arizona, Utah, Nevada, California, Oregon and Washington Territories. It may be designated as comprising 17 degrees of latitude, or a breadth of eleven hundred miles, from north to south, and of nearly equal longitudinal extension, making an area of more than a million of square miles.

" This vast region is traversed from north to south, first, on the Pacific side, by the Sierra Nevada and Cascade Mountains, then by the Blue and Humboldt; on the east, by the double ranges of the Rocky Mountains, embracing the Wasatch and Wind River Chain, and the Sierra Madre, stretching longitudinally and in lateral spurs, crossed and linked together by intervening ridges, connecting the whole system by five principal ranges, dividing the country into an equal number of basins, each being nearly surrounded by mountains, and watered by mountain streams and snows, thereby interspersing this immense territory with bodies of agricultural lands, equal to the support, not only of miners, but of a dense population.

" These mountains, are literally stocked with minerals; gold and silver being interspersed in profusion over this immense surface, and daily brought to light by new discoveries. In addition to the deposits of gold and silver,

the Indian Ocean, and of all the valleys which are drained by the rivers of Africa and Europe which empty into the Mediterranean, does not cover an extent of territory as great as that included in the valleys drained by the American rivers alone which discharge themselves into one central sea—the Gulf of Mexico."

various sections of the whole region are rich in precious stones, marble, gypsum, salt, tin, quicksilver, asphaltum, coal, iron, copper, lead, mineral and medicinal, thermal and cold springs and streams.

"The yield of the precious metals alone of this region will not fall below one hundred millions of dollars the present year, and it will augment with the increase of population, for centuries to come. Within ten years the annual product of these mines will reach two hundred millions of dollars in the precious metals, and in coal, iron, tin, lead, quicksilver and copper, half that sum. (He proposes to subject these minerals to a Government tax of eight per cent., and counts upon a revenue from this source of twenty-five millions per annum, almost immediately, and upon a proportionate increase in the future. With an amount of labor relatively equal to that expended in California,) applied to the gold fields already known to exist outside of that State, the production of this year, including that of California, would exceed four hundred millions. In a word, the value of these mines is absolutely incalculable."

The copper mines of Lake Superior, the lead and iron mines of Missouri, and the mineral productions of various other States, including the exhaustless salt springs in various parts of our country, are sources of incalculable wealth. No people on the globe possesses to a similar extent, these great sources of wealth and of revenue.

(7.) Our coast and shore line, according to Professor Bache, is in all 122,784 miles. No nation, not even all the nations of Europe combined, has such facilities for cheap water communication. Our commercial tonnage in the year 1860 was 5,358,808 tons, and our commercial fleets on oceans, lakes and rivers numbered nearly 30,000 vessels; the increase in the decade from 1850 to 1860 was over 50 per cent.; and though the war of the rebellion has temporarily retarded the progress of this branch of industry, the termination of that war will at once witness its restoration to more than its wonted prosperity.

(8.) Our manufactories and mechanical branches of industry are on an equally extensive scale with the commercial and agricultural, and are equally reliable sources of wealth to our people and of revenue to our Government. According to reliable statements, the value of our manufactured articles in 1860 exceeded $1,500,000,000.*

It is thus manifest that we are *abundantly able* to bear the burden of our national war debt, assuming it to amount even to

* I take pleasure in acknowledging my indebtedness for this valuable information, as to the power and resources of our country, to the report made on the 11th of September, 1863, to the "International Statistical Congress" at Berlin, by Samuel B. Ruggles, the delegate to that body from the United States. This report is an honor to its author and to our country. Much interesting information on this subject is also contained in a report made

$4,000,000,000 ; that we can with honorable punctuality, without impoverishment or distress, pay the interest and *can*, when necessary, pay the principal. It ought however to be mentioned that, if we are to judge by the experience of England, our public creditors, domestic or foreign, instead of requiring payment of the principal, would regard it as a serious misfortune to be compelled to receive it, so long as they had implicit confidence in the payment of the interest.

Such being our *ability*, shall we *fulfill* our solemn obligations? Patriotism, honor, morality, duty, love of republican liberty, " a decent respect for the opinions of mankind," the very instincts of national preservation unitedly and loudly answer, Yes ! This debt will have been contracted for a sacred purpose, namely, the *salvation of the national life;* it will subserve the best and most glorious of ends, namely, the preservation of our thrice blessed Government and Union and their transmission to posterity and the consequent demonstration to the world of the stability and permanence, as well as of the beauty and beneficence, of our political institutions. No patriotic man will, no well informed man has a right to, doubt that the people of the "Great Republic" will bear this burden with manly and cheerful firmness. It is a duty we owe to the memory of those who prepared for us our heritage of civil and religious freedom. It is a still more sacred and imperative duty to the tens of thousands of patriot heroes who have offered up their lives for us in this contest; their costly offerings will have been wholly in vain, if we, who survive and for whom the sacrifice was made, shall prove recreant to our duty and thus render unavailing the noble work they have, with such sublime self-devotion, performed for us. I say " render unavailing," for the disregard of our national obligations, by the repudiation of our national debt, would, of necessity involve the dissolution of our Government and the end of our national career. No nation would, no nation should, be permitted to exist under such a load of dishonor and of infamy; and that dishonor and that infamy voluntarily assumed, imposed by no necessity and admitting of no justification or even extenuation. The repudiation of that debt, or what is equivalent, the failure to

on the 12th of May, 1864, to the Union League Club of the City of New York, by a Committee on "Emigration." The report has been published. No intelligent American can rise from the perusal of the documents mentioned in this note, without the cheering conviction of the perfect ability of his country to pay the whole debt she may incur in suppressing the rebellion.

pay annually its interest, and ultimately its principal, would be deliberate *national suicide.*

Is this people prepared for that? Is it prepared to make itself the scorn of the world, the jest and the jeer of tyrants and of despots, an object of contempt and loathing to patriots in every land; to become the base betrayers of the great trust committed to them by the Almighty, heartless ingrates to the men of the Revolution who established, and to the men of this war who saved, the Republic!! And all this, too, for considerations merely *mercenary.* It cannot be believed that the "American people" will ever be guilty of an infamy whose parallel could nowhere be found; nor is it to be believed, that the revolutionary and fatal sentiments on this subject, put forth in the publication whose title is mentioned in a preceding note, will be received other than with stern reprobation by all who desire the preservation of the Union. This unspeakable calamity of repudiation *may* befall us, but *never* till the people of the United States are ready to sacrifice concurrently the Constitution and the Union; to declare that they no longer desire Republican Government and are willing to encounter the terrors of anarchy or of despotism! These results would be inevitable concomitants. Then indeed would be chanted the death song of civil liberty, and then would come the triumph of tyrants and oppressors throughout the world.

But I see in the future no such appalling spectacle. On the contrary, I look forward with unwavering confidence to the fidelity of this people to the Constitution and the Union, to their performance, as citizens of the Republic, of all things requisite to its preservation. Deeply imbued with this conviction, I cannot but see a splendid future for my country, a future filled with glory and honor and happiness; a future abounding in good, not only to us and to our posterity, but to millions from other lands, who will resort to ours in quest of peace, security, and personal and political independence which are denied them in the places of their nativity. Why should it not be so? We have had many trials as a people; through suffering and tribulation we were born as a nation; we endured much before that birth was fully consummated by the Constitution; and after that event, we had occasional afflictions up to the time of what is well denominated "The Great Rebellion." In passing through this triumphantly, we shall indeed have passed through the "fiery furnace;" but as I humbly trust and firmly believe only to be "purified;" to be made more sensible of our blessings; to be the better qualified to appreciate and enjoy them. We shall come out of the trial with a deep and enduring feeling of gratitude to the Great Disposer of events for his mercies to us, and with a heartfelt and earnest realization of the truth that "Whom the Lord *loveth* he chasteneth," and that though "no chastening for the present seemeth to be joyous but grievous, nevertheless afterwards it yieldeth the peaceable fruits of righteousness unto them, *which are exercised thereby.*" I say this in all reverence, for I acknowledge an over-ruling Providence alike in the affairs of nations and of individual man. He has subjected us in all parts of our country to this great tribulation for our good. The States in rebellion have suffered all the evils of war in their midst, desolation, destitution of the comforts and often of the necessaries of life, impoverishment, the laying waste frequently of town and country, public and private bankruptcy, hundreds of thousands of lives sacrificed or rendered useless by wounds or disease. In the States not in rebellion, innumerable firesides rendered desolate by the victims offered up in the contest, not a town or neighborhood that has not lost some or many loved ones; patriot heroes of all ages yielded up to death in the battle-field or in the hospital; a national debt of extraordinary magnitude devolved upon the nation. Though they have not within their own borders, except to a very limited extent, had the frightful experience of actual war; and though, as I have before remarked, a stranger in passing through our States would scarcely be aware that war existed; and though our material prosperity, public and individual, has not been sensibly affected, yet millions of individuals among us have been called on to weep in bitter, inconsolable anguish. Thus, everywhere through the land, has the hand of affliction been laid heavily on the people. Thus, as individuals and as communities, both sections of our land have had enough to awaken them to solemn and sober reflection, and to expose to their view their errors and sins as a nation and as men and to lead them to better purposes for the future. In vain will have been those severe chastisements, unless those results follow.

Under the subduing and softening influence of this awfully impressive lesson, the patriot and the Christian may well hope, that the American people will, for a long time to come, study to avoid the errors of the past; to seek higher, purer aims; to cultivate the feelings of kindly brotherhood, and to diffuse everywhere among us the spirit of a true Christian civilization.

I believe that the lesson will not be lost upon us, and that we shall emerge from this contest a better and a purer, a more patriotic and a more unselfish people; more deeply sensible of the value of our institutions; more grateful to God for the blessings he has in them vouchsafed to us.

Thus, I see at no distant period the extinction of the rebellion and the restoration of every State to its wonted place in our happy Union; and then lies before us a more brilliant prospect than has yet been placed before any people. It may be termed the beginning of a new career. We start upon it with the respect and admiration of the world for the wonderful works we have done; the power— physical, moral and financial—we have displayed; the sublime ex- hibitions of individual heroism and courage which have been so profusely abundant both at the South and the North; the manifes- tation of a high civilization in so many deeds of charity, benevo- lence and philanthropy. Every nation will award to us the proud and coveted title of a *brave* people. We start upon this career, too, with deeper devotion to our country and more exalted con- ceptions of its destiny and its mission. We enter upon it with the perfect conviction that, whatever may have been the fact hereto- fore, the events of the last three years will have conclusively dem- onstrated that we are for ever safe, by means of our military genius and power, if for no other reason, from *foreign* intrusion or attack, and consequently that we can pursue undisturbed the arts of peace and cherish all that can elevate us as men and as a nation. Our population and territorial extent, our national resources and rapid and certain increase, our Constitution, that work of surpassing wisdom, entirely adequate as it is to the safe and happy govern- ment, in a national sense, of the millions that will occupy our terri- tory; our State Governments so beautifully adapted to the purposes for which they were designed, and between which and the General Government there never can be any discordance except such as may arise from the unhallowed ambition of wicked men; all these entitle us to look forward to a future alike illustrious and benefi- cent.

The terrible lesson taught by the rebellion, originating as it did from the unhallowed ambition just mentioned, will, let us trustfully hope, secure us for centuries to come against a recurrence of the calamity.

In reference to the other peoples of the world, " we are set as a beacon on a hill." To such as now enjoy the blessings of civilization and Christianity we merely offer our political system as an example worthy of imitation; but we interfere with none and are in no sense propagandists.

As to those yet in the darkness of heathenism and without our civilization, our mission is, by humane and peaceful means, to carry to them a knowledge of the *truth* in its highest sense and thus ultimately to lead them out of the dark paths, in which they are groping, into the bright ways of knowledge, liberty and Christianity.

Without vain boasting or any assumption of superiority, we have a right to feel and to say that "our lines are cast in pleasant places;" that the Great Lord of all has given us a "goodly heritage," and we may humbly and gratefully believe that it will not be taken from us, except through our own wickedness, waywardness or folly.